Joel was stu...
reaction to he...

Over the years he ... every emotion it was possible to feel for the opposite sex—*except love, of course*—but he'd never felt this overwhelming need to protect a woman before.

Until now.

But with Lucy looking up at him with those huge green eyes he suddenly understood why his brother had been so ridiculously protective of her. There was something about her. A gentleness—*a vulnerability*—that made you want to hunt for a dragon just so that you could slay it.

Sarah Morgan trained as a nurse and has since worked in a variety of health-related jobs. Married to a gorgeous businessman who still makes her knees knock, she spends most of her time trying to keep up with their two little boys but manages to sneak off occasionally to indulge her passion for writing romance. Sarah loves outdoor life and is an enthusiastic skier and walker. Whatever she is doing, her head is always full of new characters and she is addicted to happy endings.

Recent titles by the same author:

THE DOCTOR'S ENGAGEMENT
EMERGENCY: MOTHER WANTED
THE PLAYBOY DOCTOR
THE DOCTOR'S RUNAWAY BRIDE

THE SEDUCTION CHALLENGE

BY
SARAH MORGAN

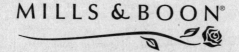

MILLS & BOON®

First published in Great Britain 2003
Harlequin Mills & Boon Limited,
Eton House, 18-24 Paradise Road, Richmond, Surrey TW9 1SR

© Sarah Morgan 2003

ISBN 0 263 83421 2

Set in Times Roman 10½ on 12 pt.
03-0103-48379

Printed and bound in Spain
by Litografía Rosés, S.A., Barcelona

CHAPTER ONE

'PLEASE, Mrs Lambert,' Lucy coaxed gently, 'just try it for me?'

'But I've hardly any breath now, dear,' the old lady wheezed. 'How can I possibly puff into that? It'll kill me!'

Lucy held the peak-flow meter and smiled. 'Just breathe in and then blow out sharply, like this…' She gave a quick demonstration and changed the mouthpiece. 'Now you have a go.'

'But why?' Mrs Lambert took the device from Lucy and looked at it doubtfully. 'I don't understand.'

'This little machine helps us to measure how well your lungs are.' Lucy explained patiently, nothing in her manner betraying the fact that this was the fourth time she'd given the same explanation to the old woman.

'Oh.' Mrs Lambert looked surprised. 'Well, why didn't you say so before?'

Lucy smothered a smile and pulled the top off her pen ready to record the results. 'Blow when you're ready, Mrs Lambert.'

Behind her the door opened and she turned to see Richard Whittaker, the senior partner, hovering in the doorway. Grey-haired and kindly, he looked at Mrs Lambert and gave a discreet thumbs-up sign. Lucy smiled and read the result of the peak-flow meter.

'Well done, Mrs Lambert,' she said warmly. 'Twice more now. I need the best of three.'

'Three? I'll be in my grave, girl!' Mrs Lambert looked

horrified and turned to Richard with a small smile. 'She's a slave-driver, this new nurse of yours.'

'I know.' Richard Whittaker folded his arms across his chest and leaned against the door, his expression sympathetic. 'We all suffer, I'm afraid. She bullies us unmercifully. I should just give in, if I were you. That's what we doctors do.'

Mrs Lambert gave a dramatic sigh and then blew sharply into the meter.

Lucy recorded the results and handed them to Richard with a pleased smile. 'They're not bad. Especially considering all the talking you've done since you came in here...' she gave the old lady a teasing wink and Mrs Lambert laughed.

'You're a cheeky girl!'

Richard studied the results and then glanced up. 'She's right, you know. These results are good, Annie. We've been monitoring them regularly now, which helps us make a decision about your treatment. I don't think we need alter anything at the moment but make sure you keep using the puffers.'

Annie Lambert's mouth tightened. 'I really don't see why I need to. I feel fine.'

'You have asthma, Mrs Lambert. You feel fine because you've been taking your puffers,' Lucy explained, and the old lady sighed.

'It's a load of nonsense. How can I have asthma? I'm seventy years old, for goodness' sake. Children get asthma, not adults!'

'Adults get it too, Annie.' Richard gave her a worried look. 'We've explained it before, but we'll explain it again if—'

'No, no—' Annie Lambert interrupted him with an impatient gesture. 'You keep going on about puffers and blowing and all sorts of nonsense. I don't want to listen to it any more. It's boring.'

Lucy smiled. 'It is pretty boring, isn't it? And the good thing about remembering to take your puffers is that they keep you well so that you can then forget about the fact that you have asthma.'

'I take the one regularly,' Annie said primly, picking up her handbag and slipping it onto her arm. 'And then the other one when I'm in a spot of trouble, but I must admit I feel pretty breathless sometimes.'

'That's as much your heart condition as your asthma,' Richard explained gently, handing the chart back to Lucy. 'We've increased the dose of your tablets now, so hopefully that should do the trick.'

'I hope so,' Annie said, her smile slightly tired, 'or there's no way I'll be running the marathon next year.'

'You'll be the first over the finishing line,' Lucy teased gently, her eyes twinkling as she helped the old lady into the waiting room. 'Bye, Mrs Lambert. I'll see you next month unless you need me before that.'

She walked back to the treatment room, surprised to find Richard still there.

'She's doing well, isn't she?' She pulled the mouthpiece out of the peak-flow meter and tossed it in the bin, carefully placing the device back on her asthma tray ready for the next time it would be needed.

Richard adjusted his metal-rimmed glasses and nodded. 'Amazingly so. You're a miracle-worker. I could never persuade her to blow into ''that infernal machine'', as she calls it. Your asthma clinic works a treat.'

Lucy smiled briefly, embarrassed by the praise. 'It's only because I have more time than you.'

Richard snorted. 'No, it's not! Sometimes I think you're the busiest person in the place. You've got the touch, that's all,' he said softly, his eyes suddenly searching as he looked at her. 'But I didn't really want to talk about Annie Lambert. I wanted to talk about you. You've been with us for a month now. I want to know how you are.'

Lucy gave him a grateful smile. 'I'm fine,' she said quietly, touched that he cared enough to ask.

'Fine?' Richard gave a curious smile and walked across the room to stare out of the window. 'Do you know, I've decided over the years that I hate that word?' he observed. 'It doesn't say anything about how a person is really feeling.'

Lucy stared at him, wondering what else to say.

She certainly couldn't tell him the truth. That deep inside she hurt so badly she could barely breathe. That she was lonely and sad and that sometimes her fear of the future was so intense it threatened to choke her.

She'd felt that way for a whole year, ever since—

With a sigh, she pushed the memories away. She'd long since made it a rule not to think about her problems at work, but if the senior partner was asking how she was then maybe she wasn't doing such a great job at hiding her feelings.

Or maybe something else was the matter...

A flicker of anxiety ran through her insides. 'Is something wrong?' She searched her mind for possibilities. 'I know it's awkward for you that I have to finish work at three, and—'

'Lucy, Lucy—' Richard interrupted her gently, and walked slowly towards her, a frown creasing his forehead. 'Let's get one thing straight, shall we? Your contribution to this practice is immeasurable. None of us care about you having to finish work at three. I'm not asking how you are because I have any professional concerns. My interest was completely personal. Elizabeth is worried about you and frankly so am I.'

He ran his eyes over her quickly and his mouth tightened. 'You look tired. Are you having trouble sleeping?'

She opened her mouth to deny it and then realised the futility of it. The man was a doctor, for goodness' sake.

'Sometimes,' she hedged, 'but I'm all right, truly. I love it here.'

It was true—she did love it.

Moving to this pretty part of Cornwall was the best thing that had happened to her in a long time.

Richard's eyes narrowed. 'You know, I could give you something to help with the sleeping.'

'No.' She shook her head, horrified at the suggestion. 'Thank you, but, no. I prefer not to.'

What was the point?

The sadness would still be there when she woke up.

Hoping to change the subject, she picked up a dressing pack and tidied it away in the cupboard. 'By the way, those new dressing packs we ordered are great. Much less wastage than the old ones. It should save the practice a significant amount of money in the long run.'

'Lucy, I don't care about the dressing packs!' Richard ran both hands through his hair in frustration. 'Well, I do care, of course,' he corrected himself quickly, 'but not at the moment. Stop working and sit down, will you? I can't talk to you while you're moving around the room.'

Resigning herself to the fact that he wasn't going to let the subject drop, Lucy did as she was told.

'How are you finding the flat?'

'Fantastic,' she replied immediately. 'I've never lived anywhere so beautiful.'

It was true. After living in a cramped, damp flat in the

grey suburbs of London, the spacious, airy flat with views over the harbour was straight out of her fantasies.

Richard adjusted his glasses and peered at her. 'But you're not meeting people.'

'I meet people through my work,' she pointed out quickly, and he gave a wry smile.

'That isn't exactly what I meant.'

She stared down at her hands, wondering why it was that everyone thought that the cure for a broken relationship was a new one. 'I know what you meant and believe me when I say that meeting men isn't high on my list of priorities at the moment.'

And she couldn't imagine that it ever would be.

He nodded slowly. 'I can understand why you feel that way, but give it time, Lucy, and you'll feel differently. Sooner or later you need to get out there and build a new life.'

Did she?

How?

She had no experience in starting relationships. She'd known Tim since she was six years old and had always assumed that one day they'd get married. She'd just never imagined that it wouldn't last for ever.

The whole concept of meeting and dating men—*strangers*—was completely alien to her.

'I wish you'd join Elizabeth and me for a meal one day,' Richard was saying. 'We'd love to have you.'

Lucy smiled gently. 'Dr Whittaker, you have been un-believably kind to me since we met. I was a total stranger to you but you gave me a part-time job when you needed a full-time nurse, and you let me have a flat rent-free—'

'You're doing us a favour, living in it during the winter. There are no tourists at this time of year,' Richard reminded her, 'so it's sitting empty.'

Lucy fiddled with the material of her uniform. 'What I mean is that you've been extraordinarily generous. You don't need to feed me as well.'

He frowned. 'But you do cook for yourself in the evening?'

'Oh, yes,' she said quickly, wondering if cereal and toast counted as cooking. It didn't matter. She owed the Whittakers so much already, she certainly didn't intend to impose on their kindness any more than she had to.

Richard looked at her regretfully. 'Well, if you change your mind, you only have to ask. By the way, I wanted to remind you that my younger son is arriving today. I did mention that he would be joining the practice?'

'Several times.' Relieved that he'd changed the subject, Lucy hooked a strand of dark hair behind her ear and hid a smile. Richard's pride in his youngest son was obvious to all. 'I can't believe all three of your sons are doctors.'

'And they've all descended on my practice!' Richard pulled a sorrowful face but Lucy knew that it was just for show. The Whittakers were closer than any family she'd ever met, and even in the brief time that she'd worked for them she'd seen that having a family practice worked well. Michael and Nick, the two sons she'd been working with for the past month, were both skilled doctors and clearly respected each other. There was none of the rivalry and pettiness that was reputed to taint other practices.

'So when does your youngest son start officially?'

'As soon as he sets foot inside the door,' Richard said dryly. 'We're rushed off our feet, as you know. He's arriving just in time for the flu season. Anyway, I'll introduce you as soon as he arrives because he'll be doing quite a few of the clinics with you. What are you doing at lunchtime? Are you around?'

Lucy hesitated, not sure whether to confess or not. 'Actually, I'm going to see Ivy Williams,' she said finally, honesty prevailing, as always. 'I'm really worried about her. I saw her last week to dress her leg and she was very quiet. People keep telling me that since Bert died a month ago she's barely left the house.'

That was the advantage of a small community, she reflected. There was always someone who was going to notice that you were in trouble.

'Ivy?' Richard's face softened but his eyes were concerned. 'That's kind of you, but don't get too involved, Lucy. You can't solve everyone's problems.'

'I know that,' Lucy said, her green eyes gentle and kind. 'But she's lost her partner and she must be so lost and lonely…'

And she knew only too well how that felt.

'Well, let me know how she is,' Richard said, walking towards the door and giving her a smile. 'You're a kind girl, Lucy, and we're lucky to have you.'

But nowhere near as lucky as she was to have them.

Lucy watched Richard go and then grabbed her coat and made her way across the car park, noticing with relief that someone had sprinkled grit on the surface. Just as well, she reflected, shivering as the cold air numbed her cheeks and fingers, otherwise all their patients would be slipping and sliding and breaking bones before they reached the surgery.

Even for early January it was bitterly cold, and she blew on her hands to warm them and forced her mind back to her work.

What was she going to do about Ivy? She was truly worried about her, rattling around in that big house on her own.

The problem nagged her brain as she drove carefully along the coast road, and she was still thinking about it when she heard a hideous squeal of tyres followed by a sickening crash.

What…?

Instinctively she pumped her brake pedal, slowing her car gradually as she approached the bend in the road.

There'd been an accident.

She rounded the corner, her heart racing as she braced herself for what she might see.

Her fingers tightened on the wheel and she started to shake as she saw the twisted wreckage of a car embedded in a tree. And then she saw the motorbike.

'Oh, no…'

Her heart thumping uncontrollably, she pulled her car over onto the grass verge, put on her hazard warning lights and sprinted across to the wreckage. The front of the car was badly mangled, and next to it lay a pile of twisted metal that had once been a motorbike. She was shaking with reaction as she looked frantically for the rider.

Where was he?

She muttered a denial as she finally located his body metres away in the grass. How could he possibly have survived?

Staring in horror at his still body, she felt panic numb her brain and for precious seconds she stood frozen, unable to move a muscle. But then the cold winter air flowed under her coat, bringing her to her senses.

After the sickening noise of the crash the air was still and silent, and it was as if she were the only person in the whole world.

But fortunately she wasn't.

Sounds of a car approaching cut through the frozen silence and Lucy waved her arms frantically as it appeared round the bend.

The car slowed and then came to a halt and a young couple climbed out, picking their way along the icy road

Seeing the danger immediately, Lucy sprinted towards them, her feet slipping on the frozen tarmac. 'Reverse your car!'

The man looked at her blankly and the woman just stared in horror at the mangled motorbike, her hand over her mouth.

Lucy gestured towards the road. 'This is a blind bend,' she said urgently, 'And there are obviously patches of black ice. If anyone else comes round here too fast there'll be another accident. Reverse your car and put the hazard warning lights on so that people will see you and slow down.'

'Gotcha.' The young man suddenly seemed to pull himself together and dashed back to do as Lucy had ordered.

Aware that the next priority was to summon help, she pulled her mobile phone out of her pocket and rammed it into the young woman's hand.

'We need to get some help fast. Take a deep breath,' Lucy ordered firmly, hoping she sounded more in control than she felt. 'I'm a nurse and I'll deal with the accident, but I need you to call 999. Can you do that? Give them our location and tell them that there's a car and a motorbike involved.'

The woman nodded mutely and Lucy gave her shoulder a squeeze.

'Good. Quickly, then...'

Feeling slightly better, knowing that help would soon be on the way, she ran back towards the car, hoping that she wouldn't have to hold the fort by herself for long.

One glance into the car showed her that there was just the driver and one passenger.

'Tell them two in the car,' she yelled over her shoulder,

hoping that the young woman had managed to contact the ambulance service.

Although the doors had been jammed in the crash, she managed to shout through the windows.

'Get us out! Get us out!' The woman was clawing frantically at the door and Lucy glanced over her shoulder to the still figure of the motorcyclist, trying to remember what she'd learned about triage. Surely he had to be her priority. The two in the car were conscious. Or was he beyond help? In which case, she needed to rescue the two in the car.

With a whimper of panic she turned back to the couple in the car and gestured to the sun roof, suggesting that they try and open it. Then she turned her attention to the motorcyclist.

She had to assess his injuries. If he was dead, then the couple in the car became the priority, but if he wasn't...

Oh, please, God, don't let him be dead.

Her heart thumping, her feet crunched on the frozen grass and she dropped to her knees next to his body, trying to subdue the panic that was bubbling up inside her. It had been years since she'd done any A and E work and even then it had only been when she'd been training. But she knew the principles, she reminded herself firmly. ABC. Airway, breathing, circulation.

The cold from the ground oozed up and numbed her knees, but she didn't even notice.

'The ambulance is on its way.' The young man was back by her side. 'Here, let me help you take his helmet off.'

'No!' Lucy reached out a hand to stop him touching the injured motorcyclist, her voice sharper than she'd intended. 'You should never remove the helmet unless breathing is compromised. The helmet is supporting his neck and if we take it off...'

She wasn't qualified to help this man.

She was a practice nurse, for goodness' sake, not a paramedic.

Airway—she had to check his airway.

She leaned closer and just at that moment the man groaned and muttered something.

Lucy let out a long breath. *He was talking.* Surely that had to be a good sign?

'Hello? Can you tell me where it hurts?'

She cringed as she listened to herself. What a stupid question to ask someone who'd been thrown from a bike. It probably hurt everywhere...

'Leg.'

Leg.

Lucy ran her eyes down his legs and saw the nasty gash in the leathers and the mass of blood gathering there. She wrenched off her gloves and thrust them into her pocket, her fingers shifting the leathers so that she could take a closer look.

Blood spurted into the air.

'Oh, no!' She pressed down on the leg hard and turned to the man from the car, noticing that he was looking slightly green. She felt slightly green, too. She'd never seen such a severe laceration. Despite the protection of the leathers, his thigh had been badly torn, presumably because he'd been thrown across the tarmac. 'You need to go to my car, quickly. Fetch the bag on the back seat.'

'And don't pass out on me,' she muttered under her breath as she watched him go.

The motorcyclist moaned again and tried to move.

'Try and keep still,' Lucy said urgently, wishing that she could hold his hand to reassure him. Unfortunately, both her hands were occupied in preventing him from bleeding to death. 'You're going to be just fine. I'm a nurse and there's an ambulance on the way. Everything is going to be fine…'

She said it to reassure herself as much as him, and she reflected briefly on the ridiculous things people said when they were trying to reassure each other.

Everything was far from fine.

'Here's your bag.' The young man was back beside her, looking at her expectantly.

She almost laughed aloud. Did he expect her bag to contain magic powers?

Weighed down by the knowledge that everyone was depending on her, she glanced over her shoulder towards the road, desperately praying that the ambulance would arrive quickly, but there was nothing but an eerie winter silence.

Which meant that the man's life depended on her and the very inadequate contents of her practice nurse's bag.

Lucy glanced down at her hands, which were slippery with the man's blood. There was no way she could let go.

'Inside the side pockets you'll find some sterile dressing pads,' she instructed, noticing that underneath the helmet the injured man was ghostly pale. He was losing a lot of blood and needed some fluids fast.

And she didn't have any—what else should she do?

Elevate the bleeding part—but what with?

This situation was way beyond her experience. And well beyond a few dressing pads.

Where on earth was the ambulance?

Her heart still thudding, Lucy snatched the pads from the young man and pressed down on the wound again.

'There should be a bandage in there, too,' she muttered. She had to stem the bleeding and she really ought to take another look at the two in the car.

'Do you need help?'

The deep voice came from behind her and she turned her head, blinking at the raw, male power of the man in front of her. Black leathers outlined broad, muscular shoulders and long, powerful legs. Another motorcyclist?

He dragged off his helmet, revealing cropped dark hair and a pair of cool blue eyes that took in the situation in one glance. He dropped to his haunches and his face was close enough for her to see the dark growth shadowing the line of his hard jaw. He obviously hadn't shaved recently. She frowned at her own thoughts and shook herself. Someone's life was at risk and she was wondering when this man had last shaved?

Was she going completely mad?

It must be the shock.

'Did you see it happen?' His sharp tone brought her quickly back to the present and she shook her head.

'No. But from the damage to the front of the car I guess it must have hit him.' She tried to stop her teeth chattering. 'The roads are very icy.'

Those cool blue eyes flickered to the car, his expression serious. 'How many in the car?'

'Two.'

'Have you checked them?'

'Briefly.' Lucy responded without question to the authority in his voice. 'They were both shouting and yelling so I thought that this man seemed more urgent.'

Dear God, she hoped she'd done the right thing. Her first aid was very rusty. What if the people in the car died because of her?

But this motorcyclist would definitely die if she moved her hands.

She swallowed. 'This man has got a nasty laceration on his thigh and he's bleeding from an artery. Oh, God, look…' She stared helplessly at the pads under her fingers, which were already soaked through with blood. 'What do we do?'

'You keep pressing while I elevate the limb…' The man wedged something under the injured leg and then briefly examined the young man with a skill and confidence that left her in no doubt as to his profession.

'You're a doctor,' she mumbled with relief, and he gave her a brief smile.

'For my sins.' His gaze returned to the injured man. 'This chap needs fluids urgently. How long ago did you call the ambulance?'

Lucy bit her lip. 'About five minutes? We phoned immediately.'

'They ought to use the helicopter,' he muttered, shifting his position slightly. 'Why don't you check the couple in the car again?' He glanced up at the young man, who was still hovering. 'Can you take over here and press on the wound? That would leave us free to check on the others.'

Lucy opened her mouth to point out that the man had turned pale green at the sight of all the blood, but the doctor was already halfway through demonstrating the first aid for an arterial bleed, his tone brisk and matter-of-fact as he talked. His cool confidence seemed to have a positive effect on the driver and he was soon nodding agreement and preparing to take over from Lucy.

Relieved that someone who clearly knew what he was doing was now in charge, she swapped places with the other man and looked ruefully down at her hands.

'There's a water bottle on my bike.' The blue eyed doctor had noticed her predicament and she smiled at him gratefully.

Seconds later she had cleaned up as best she could and was dealing with the people in the car.

The woman passenger had already dragged herself out through the sun roof and was sitting on the grass verge, blood trickling from a wound in her scalp. Judging that she was obviously not in immediate danger, Lucy turned her attentions to the driver.

After tugging at the door without success, she climbed onto the bonnet and talked to him through the sun roof.

'Can you tell me where it hurts?'

The man groaned, his face chalk-white. 'My legs.'

Lucy squinted down into the footwell, but the twisted metal stopped her seeing anything. 'Can you wiggle your toes? Yes or no?'

'Yes.'

Well, that was something, but there was still always the risk that he'd damaged his spine.

'How are we doing here?' The doctor was suddenly by her side, his gaze calm and appraising as he looked at her. How could he be so cool about the whole situation? Her insides were totally knotted.

'His legs are trapped, but he's got feeling,' she told him, sliding off the bonnet and straightening her clothes quickly. 'But I'm worried about his neck and I can't get the door open. The passenger climbed out through the sun roof.'

'We'll deal with him first, then,' the doctor murmured, taking a firm grip of the doorhandle and bracing his broad shoulders. 'Let's see what we can do about the door, shall we?'

Planting his foot on the car to give him extra leverage, he gave the door a powerful yank and it groaned open reluctantly. Noting the swell of muscle under his leathers, Lucy wondered how on earth she would have managed if he hadn't come along. There was no way she could have opened that door.

Having sorted out the door, he squatted down beside the injured man, asked a few questions and then straightened up again.

Lucy looked at him anxiously. 'Wh—what do you want me to do? Should we get him out?'

'No way.' The doctor shook his head decisively. 'We need to immobilise his spine. We'll leave him there until the ambulance arrives and we can get our hands on a spinal board.'

Lucy's gaze skidded towards the car and she lowered her voice. 'What if the car catches fire?'

His blue eyes gleamed slightly. 'You've been watching too many movies. It does happen, of course, but very rarely, and the car seems OK in this case. We'll keep an eye on it but I don't want to move him until we can get some support on that neck. It's the only part of him that's really worrying me.'

Lucy wondered what it must be like to have so much self-confidence. He didn't seem at all daunted by the emergency situation they were facing. He just assessed each problem as it came along and dealt with it.

He pulled back the sleeve of his jacket and glanced at his watch. 'OK—well, we've done just about everything we can with limited equipment. What we need now is an ambulance.'

Looking at the grim set of his mouth, Lucy gave a little shiver and decided that she wouldn't want to be on the wrong side of him. There was no denying that he was staggeringly handsome, but there was something intimidating about the breadth of his muscular shoulders and the ruthless set of his dark jaw.

And then they both heard the clack, clack, clack of an approaching helicopter and he glanced towards her and gave her a wink and a smile that made her insides turn over. He had the sexiest smile she'd ever seen and suddenly the rhythm of her breathing was totally disrupted. When he smiled like that it softened his appearance and he no longer looked rough and aggressively male. Just plain handsome.

Lucy looked away from him, confused by her reaction to him. She couldn't remember the last time she'd noticed that a man was handsome.

Maybe it was a good sign.

Maybe she was slowly starting to recover from everything that had happened.

Strong fingers gripped her arm and held her firmly. 'Stay well back while they land.'

She did as she was told, responding automatically to the cool authority in his tone. She had no intention of arguing with him. As far as she was concerned there'd been no question as to who'd been in charge from the moment he'd stepped off his motorbike.

Lucy watched in fascination as the helicopter hovered and the pilot landed with breathtaking skill. She'd heard about the air ambulance of course, but this was the first time she'd actually seen it in action.

Two paramedics ran from the helicopter and one of them grinned in surprise when he saw the doctor.

'Joel? I thought we'd got rid of you, mate!'

'So did I,' the doctor replied, his tone dry, 'but someone up there obviously thought differently. The motorcyclist needs a line in fast, Greg. Let's get some Hartmann's into him, and for goodness' sake make it warm or we'll kill him off. And grab a Hudson mask because he needs ninety percent oxygen. You'd better warn them to have three units of O-neg ready in A and E because he's going to need blood. He's our priority. We need to evacuate him before the occupants of the car.'

The paramedic called Greg nodded. 'There's an ambulance on its way—ETA three minutes. They can take the people from the car.'

'Great. Let's get to work, then.'

Lucy stood to one side, assuming that if he wanted her help he'd ask for it. He reeled off several other instructions and then strode off to deal with the motorcyclist while the second paramedic hurried up to her.

'What's the story with the guy in the car?'

'It's his neck, or at least that's what he—Joel.' She stumbled over the name. 'Joel is worried about. He thinks it should be immobilised before he's moved.'

The paramedic nodded. 'Let's do it then. I've never known Joel be wrong.'

So the self-confidence was justified.

Lucy glanced in the direction of the doctor, who was now on his knees beside the motorcyclist, squeezing fluid into him from an IV bag. 'I can't understand how he can be so cool. I was in a total panic before he turned up.'

The paramedic gave her a sympathetic smile. 'So at a guess I'd say you're not a trauma doctor. He is.'

A trauma doctor? Well, that would explain the unshakable self-confidence.

'So that's why he wasn't fazed.'

The paramedic gave a short laugh as he handed her some equipment. 'Never seen him fazed by anything, to be honest, but some people are just like that, aren't they? We used to call him Joe Cool. One thing's for sure. If I was ever in a pile-up and I saw him hovering over me I'd know I was going to be OK. He's one hell of a clever doctor and a big loss, if you ask me.'

'Loss?' Lucy obediently held the equipment he gave her and waited to be given instructions.

'Yeah. He was working with us until two weeks ago.

Then he left for pastures new. Bloody waste. Best trauma doctor I've ever seen.'

'So why did he leave?'

The paramedic shrugged. 'He wanted a change. Fed up with being in the news, I suppose. Anyway, let's get this guy out.'

In the news?

Why was the doctor in the news?

Lucy stared at the paramedic, who gave her a friendly grin and went back to the car.

Behind her she heard the helicopter taking off again and realised that the motorcyclist was already on his way to hospital.

Her eyes widened as she realised how quickly they must have worked.

The doctor sprinted back to the car and helped the paramedic stabilise the driver while Lucy checked on his passenger.

A fire engine and an ambulance arrived and suddenly there were people everywhere. In no time at all the man was freed and he and his companion were on their way to hospital.

Suddenly Lucy found herself alone with the blue-eyed doctor.

'Well, that livened up the lunch-hour,' he drawled as they watched the ambulance race away, siren blaring.

Lucy gave a rueful smile and pushed a thick strand of dark hair out of her eyes with trembling fingers. Now that it was all over she felt slightly sick.

In fact, she felt dizzy.

The doctor must have noticed because he frowned suddenly. 'Are you OK? Damn, you're white as a sheet. Sit down fast—that's it. Head down.'

He pushed her down onto the grassy bank and guided

her head between her knees with a strong hand. She took several deep breaths and waited for the swimmy feeling to pass.

'Sorry.' She lifted her head and gave him an embarrassed look. 'I don't—'

'Don't worry about it,' he said softly, his hand still lingering on the back of her neck. 'It's the shock. You're all right while it's happening, and then when the crisis has passed it hits you. It happens to everyone.'

She was willing to bet that it had never happened to him, but she was grateful to him for trying to make her feel better.

She gave him a shaky smile, relieved that he'd forced her to sit down. She didn't think her legs were capable of holding her.

'I'm not used to dealing with emergencies by the roadside,' she confessed, her breath clouding the frozen air. 'I felt totally helpless. I hope I didn't do anything wrong. I've never panicked so much in my life. I just didn't know who to deal with first, and my first aid is so—'

'You did a good job,' he said, interrupting her gently, his eyes sharply observant as they scanned her pale features.

Shy and uncomfortable under his scrutiny, she dipped her head and her dark hair tumbled forward over her face. 'Well, I'm a nurse,' she muttered, and the man threw back his head and laughed. A rich, masculine sound that made her stomach flip over.

'I suspected that from the glimpse of your uniform under your coat and the inexhaustible supply of sterile dressing pads.' He chuckled, his eyes dancing. 'Either that or you're a stripogram, but I assumed it was a bit early in the day for that.'

Lucy smiled hesitantly, unused to exchanging banter

with strange men, but his answering smile was so warm and compelling that she started to relax.

'I'm really glad that you came along when you did,' she confessed. 'It was definitely my lucky day.'

His smile faded and his gaze was suddenly disturbingly intense. 'I'm starting to think it was my lucky day, too,' he said softly, and she felt hot colour flood into her cheeks.

Was he flirting with her?

It had been so long since anyone had flirted with her that she didn't have a clue how to respond, and she scrambled unsteadily to her feet, feeling gauche and ridiculously shy.

'I'd better go.'

She had to. She had to get away from the way he was looking at her.

He rose to his feet with the easy grace of a jungle predator and strolled with her back to her car, pausing to scoop up his discarded helmet on the way. One sideways glance confirmed just how incredibly good-looking he was and she almost laughed at herself.

Any other woman would have taken advantage of the situation and made witty conversation, but faced with all that raw masculinity all she wanted to do was run a mile.

He paused by the car and his eyes rested on her face. 'You know, you shouldn't worry. You did incredibly well back there.' His voice was deep and cultured. 'And you didn't drag off his helmet, which is what most people would have done. What sort of a nurse are you?'

Lucy blushed awkwardly, thinking that his voice matched his looks. 'Just a practice nurse.'

'Just?' His dark brows rose and his mouth tilted slightly at the corners. 'Must be a pretty lucky practice if those skills you just showed are anything to go by.'

'I—well, thanks…' Lucy had never felt so tongue-tied

in her life. It had been fine when they'd been working together, but now she was suddenly aware that they were alone and the way he was looking at her unnerved her. Not as a doctor surveying a colleague but as a man looking at a woman. And what a man...

His easy assurance made her feel awkward and out of her depth, and the strength of her reaction to him shocked her.

Tim had been her first and only boyfriend and she couldn't remember a time when he'd been intimidating. Far from it. In many ways Tim had always been the boy she'd grown up with. Familiar and comfortable.

But there was nothing familiar and comfortable about the man watching her now. Nothing remotely boyish. He was every inch a man, and his arrogant stance and the confident way he surveyed her brought her flesh out in tiny goose-bumps.

Catching the gleam in his wicked, sexy eyes, she knew instinctively that he was aware of the effect he was having on her.

'I'll wait here for the police,' he suggested, tucking his helmet under one arm and trapping her gaze with his. 'Perhaps you ought to leave me your details if you're thinking of dashing off.'

Her eyes widened and her heart leapt into her mouth. 'Why?'

His smile was slow and lazy. 'So that I can call you up and pester you, of course.'

'Oh...' His directness took her breath away and his smile widened.

'Alternatively, I could give it to the police, who are bound to want a statement.'

Flustered, she lifted a hand and scraped her dark hair out of her eyes. 'The police...'

For a moment she'd seriously thought he'd been asking her out.

He was laughing at her now, but there was warmth and something else in his gaze.

'You look about fourteen when you blush.'

She *felt* about fourteen.

'So come on, gorgeous,' he said easily, 'tell me all. Name, rank and serial number.'

Gorgeous?

No one had ever called her gorgeous before.

She opened her mouth but no sound came out.

'Look, it's easy. Just copy me.' He folded his arms across his broad chest, his eyes teasing her gently. 'I'm Joel. I'm thirty-three years old, I'm single and when I grow up I want to be a doctor. I love people and animals and what I most want is world peace. There. How hard was that? Now it's your turn.'

What should she say?

Hi, I'm Lucy and I used to be married, but I'm not any more because my husband was a total rat and he broke my heart.

Maybe not.

'Come on, let's introduce ourselves.' His tone was persuasive and he stuck out his hand. She stared at it for a moment and then stretched out her own, immediately regretting the impulse as his warm, strong fingers closed over hers. His grip was as confident and powerful as the man himself, and she felt a flutter of panic. She couldn't tell him her name. Acknowledging that he was exceptionally good-looking was one thing, but handing out names and phone numbers was completely different. It might lead to something she wasn't ready to handle.

She might not have had much experience with men in

her life, but she could see at a glance that he was way out of her league.

Jerking her hand away, she stooped to pick up her bag.

'I'd better be going. The time of the accident was 12.30. That's all I know. I didn't see anything at all. Nothing. So I'd be no use to the police.' Gabbling in her haste to get away from him, she fumbled in her pocket for her car keys, but his strong fingers closed over her arm, holding her trapped.

'Slow down.' His voice was incredibly gentle. 'Why are you running away from me?'

Her breath was coming in gasps. 'I'm not running.'

'Liar.'

'—I'm going to be late,' she stammered, finally retrieving the keys and freeing herself from his grasp.

He reached out a hand and took the keys from her, unlocking the car and opening the door so that she could slip inside.

'So why the big secret?'

She glanced at him warily. 'Secret?'

A smile touched his mouth. A slow, sexy smile that made her heart stop and her breath catch in her throat.

'Go on, give me a clue.' Joel's voice teased her senses. 'Just the first letter? E for Esmerelda? L for Lucretia?'

'L for Lucy.' The minute she'd said it she could have bitten her tongue off. She'd had no intention of telling him, but the way he was looking at her made her feel—made her feel…

'Lucy…' He repeated her name slowly and thoughtfully, not even pretending to disguise his blatant interest in her. He wanted her and he wasn't afraid to show it.

For one fleeting moment she wondered what it would be like to go out with a man like him and then she dismissed the thought quickly. *It would be scary.* There would be nothing safe or tame about him. He was one hundred per cent hot-blooded male and she had absolutely no experience of men like him. The strength of attraction between them was so powerful it warmed the freezing air around them.

'May I have my keys?' She reached out a hand, her cheeks burning as he held her gaze steadily for several seconds more before slowly handing them over.

'Look…' He hesitated, clearly searching for the right words. 'I can see I've made you nervous, and I know that this isn't exactly a conventional place to meet, but I'd really like to see you again.'

She felt as though someone had squeezed all the breath from her body. 'I can't.'

'Why not?' He shrugged his broad shoulders. 'Don't you believe in love at first sight?'

She looked at him, and her smile was filled with sadness and all the pain of the last twelve months.

'I don't believe in love at all,' she said quietly, turning the key in the ignition and driving away from him before her hormones made her do something she knew she'd regret.

CHAPTER TWO

IT WAS her.

The nurse from the car accident.

Completely amazed by his good fortune, Joel stopped dead in the doorway of the waiting room. Without the covering of her thick wool coat he was able to get a good look at her, and he ran an appreciative eye over her long legs, her ridiculously slim waist and her incredible curves.

She was the sexiest woman he'd ever seen.

His eyes narrowed and his insides clenched as he watched her face, noting the huge green eyes and the soft pink mouth. She was completely and utterly feminine and every male bone in his body reacted to her.

As he watched, she bent down to retrieve a toy from the floor and he had to stop himself groaning aloud.

She had a bottom straight out of a bad boy's dreams. A perfect, rounded curve. He'd never been able to understand why women thought thin was attractive. Personally, he hated thin. As far as he was concerned, a woman was meant to have curves. And, boy, did this one have curves...

He remembered her wistful comment about not believing in love and wondered what had happened to make her look so sad and vulnerable. After she'd made that announcement he'd let her go, all his experience with women telling him that it would be a mistake to persist.

But he'd had every intention of seeing her again.

All the way to the surgery he'd been racking his brains

31

for a way of tracking her down, but now here she was, in his father's waiting room. He couldn't believe his luck.

He was about to throw a lifetime of commitment phobia to the wind and propose to her on the spot when he heard his name.

'Dr Whittaker. Dr *Whittaker!*'

He blinked, shook himself and reluctantly dragged his eyes away from Lucy, focusing instead on the woman smiling up at him.

'Er—hello, Ros.' He bent to kiss her cheek, genuinely fond of the woman who had been his father's receptionist since he was a child. 'You look gorgeous. Nice jumper.'

He always noticed what women wore. In fact he always noticed women, full stop.

Especially when they looked like Lucy.

'Go on with you!' The receptionist blushed and lifted a hand to her hair, visibly flustered by his attention. 'You're late, Dr Whittaker. Your father and brothers were expecting you this morning.'

'Something came up.' Joel gave her a saucy wink, knowing that she'd think the worst of him, because people always did and it amused him to wind them up.

With a last regretful glance towards the nurse with the curves, who still hadn't noticed him, he followed Ros through the waiting room, along the corridor that ran past the consulting rooms and up the stairs to the staff sitting room.

'I saw you on the television, Dr Whittaker.' Ros grabbed the handrail, slightly out of breath as she negotiated the stairs. 'In fact, I have to admit I didn't miss a single episode of *Helicopter Doctor.* You were fantastic. So cool and calm and wonderfully in charge of every crisis. I could hardly believe I once changed your nappy.'

'Thanks for that reminder, Ros.' Joel's tone was dry but

his eyes gleamed with humour. 'Just as long as you don't sell any photos of me in the buff to the press...'

Ros laughed. 'What was it like, trying to work with a camera on you all the time?'

'Actually, I hardly noticed them,' Joel said truthfully. 'I just got on with the job and they hovered in the background. When you've got a patient lying in pieces after a road accident you don't exactly care who's watching.'

'But now you're giving it all up to be a GP. Do you think you'll miss all the drama?' Ros paused at the top of the stairs and Joel gave a careless shrug.

'I don't think so. Six months with the air ambulance was long enough, really. I'm ready to join the family firm.'

Particularly now he'd seen the nurse that his father had employed.

The job was looking up by the minute.

Ros smiled. 'It's your father's dream, you know. All three of his sons in practice with him.'

'Yeah, I know. We spoil him.' Joel gave her a friendly wink and then went ahead of her and pushed open the door of the staffroom.

His father and older brother had practised in an old converted house until four years before, when they'd moved into this purpose-built, architect-designed medical centre built around an impressive glass atrium, which allowed plenty of light into the building. His father, who believed in the importance of pleasant working conditions, had also insisted on a spacious, well-equipped staffroom which had stunning views over the Cornish coastline.

Both his older brothers were in the staffroom now, deep in conversation with their father.

Joel sauntered in and slung his bag down on the floor. 'I thought GPs were supposed to be having a hard life at the moment. Since when did life get this relaxed? And there was I thinking you were desperate for some help from a decent doctor...'

'Well, well—it's the prodigal son.' Richard rose to his feet, strode across the room and clapped Joel on the back. 'Better late than never. We expected you earlier. What kept you?'

Joel cleared his throat. 'Well, actually—'

'Don't you mean *who* kept him? It's bound to have been a woman. It always is.' His older brother Michael gave him a wry smile from the comfort of his chair and gestured to the coffee-pot. 'Are you in need of caffeine?'

Joel nodded. 'Yes, please, but I'll have you know I was—'

'If you're seriously joining the family firm, you're going to have to curb your social life.' His other brother Nick interrupted his attempt at an explanation, his expression mocking. 'You don't get special treatment here. You can't bunk off just because you're a film star.'

Joel's eyes gleamed with humour and he rose to the bait. He was well used to responding to his brothers' banter. He'd had thirty-three years of constant practice. He gave Nick a sympathetic look, designed to drive him mad. 'I didn't realise you'd be so jealous.'

'Me? Jealous of you?' Nick gave a disgusted snort. 'Don't be soft. As if I'd want to spend six months practising medicine with a film crew stuck up my—'

'Thank you, Nick, this is a family show.' Michael's tone was dry as he cut in and handed Joel the coffee. 'You did a good job, Joel. It was an interesting series. You almost made medicine look exciting and you've definitely got the proudest mum in Cornwall.'

'You've also got the biggest mailbag,' his father commented. 'You're certainly not going to be short of adoring women to choose from after all the exposure you've had.'

'As if he ever was. Unfortunately, most of the female sex can't see further than his pretty face.' Nick yawned, and Joel leaned broad shoulders against the wall and looked at him innocently.

'If you like, you can help me answer my mailbag.'

Nick gave him a withering look and then grinned. 'Any naughty ones?'

'Dozens.' Joel's smile was wicked. 'You just don't want to know what some women would like to do with my underwear.'

Nick gave an exaggerated shudder. 'Please! Spare us the details.' He glanced at his watch. 'Enough of this idle banter. I've got calls to make, so I'll catch up with you later.'

His father lifted his eyebrow. 'Are you and Tina joining us for supper at the house?'

Joel brightened at the prospect of a family gathering. 'Has Mum killed the fatted calf?'

'Yes, although I can't think why.' Nick stood up and gave his brother a wink to take the sting out of his words. He bent down and picked up his jacket and his bag. 'Yes, we'll be there, Dad. Tina can't wait to see Joel. Seems to think that if he's living here she can calm him down and find him a nice girl who'll cure him of his wicked ways.'

'Who says I want to be cured?' Joel's eyes gleamed. 'And I don't need Tina to find me anyone. The girl of my dreams is standing in your waiting room at this very moment.'

There was a moment's silence while they all digested this piece of information and then Michael cleared his throat.

'No way is any girl who features in your dreams, which are undoubtedly pornographic, sitting in our surgery,' he said mildly, delving into the fridge for something to eat.

'Oh, for crying out loud—no more milk. Didn't anyone remember to shop this morning? Whose turn was it?'

Nick looked sheepish. 'Er—I think maybe mine, but I had an urgent house call…'

Michael picked up the empty carton with a sigh and threw it in the bin. 'OK, so who's volunteering to go across the road to the shop?'

There was a sudden chorus of excuses and Joel rolled his eyes.

'How do you lot manage to stay so undomesticated and not starve? You're useless!' He folded his arms across his broad chest and shook his head. 'I'll go, on condition that you tell me everything I need to know about my dream woman. I've already met her once this morning and—'

There was a collective groan and then Michael spoke for all of them.

'So that's why you were late! We knew it! It was bound to be a woman.'

Joel tilted his head back and swore under his breath. 'I hope your listening skills are slightly more advanced than this when you're with patients.'

His father put a hand on his shoulder and gave his older sons a disapproving frown. 'We're listening, Joel.'

'There was an accident on the coast road,' Joel explained. 'A nasty one. I stopped to help, which is why I was late.'

Michael shook his head in total disbelief. 'What is it with you and accidents? The rest of us seem to go through life only ever seeing boils and rashes, but drama is your middle name. You attract accidents like a magnet.' He leaned back in his chair and lifted an eyebrow. 'So how did the girl of your dreams fit into this?'

'She stopped to help. In fact, she was first on the scene.'

Joel's voice was soft. 'She's a nurse. *Your* nurse. Although I didn't know that at the time.'

The room fell silent and his brothers exchanged glances.

'*Our nurse?*' His father cleared his throat. 'You mean Lucy? The woman you're talking about is our Lucy?'

'Yes.' Joel glanced between them, his gaze questioning. 'What's wrong with that?'

'Forget it. She's not your type,' Nick said slowly, his expression serious for once. 'In fact, she's definitely not your type.'

'I disagree,' Joel drawled, a strange gleam in his eye as he looked at his brother. 'From what I've seen, she's definitely my type. She's gorgeous.'

'I didn't say she wasn't gorgeous.' Nick's mouth tightened. 'She *is* gorgeous. But she's also sweet and gentle and definitely not able to cope with someone like you.'

'Surely that's up to her to decide.'

Nick shook his head. 'Don't even go there, Joel, don't even think about it.'

Unfortunately it wasn't that simple.

He'd thought about little else since he'd seen her bending over the injured motorcyclist, her cheeks pink in the frozen air and her expression troubled.

'She came here for some peace and quiet and to escape some hassle she was having,' Michael told him, his face as serious as Nick's, 'so she doesn't need any more from you.'

'Whoa! Dismount from your charger, will you?' Joel lifted a hand and looked at them curiously. He'd never seen his brothers quite so protective of anyone before. 'I don't want to give her hassle.'

'No. We know exactly what you want to give her,' Nick said shortly, walking across the room and pausing with his hand on the door, 'and you can forget it, buster. You lay one hand on her—*just one finger*—and I'll knock you out cold.'

Joel's eyes gleamed and his fists tightened by his sides. 'You mean you'll try.'

'Oh, for goodness' sake, grow up!' Richard Whittaker looked at his sons impatiently. 'Haven't the three of you got anything better to do than regress to boyhood? Nick, get on with your calls.'

Nick gave a good-natured smile and waggled his finger at his brother. 'You have been warned. Anyway, she's one of Mum's projects, so you won't be let near her.'

Nick left the room, leaving Joel to digest his last remark. A real sucker for causes, his mother was always rescuing waifs and strays—animals and people.

'What's Mum got to do with Lucy?'

'She and Dad interviewed her for the job.' Michael reached for his jacket and ran his hands through his hair. 'You know Mum. Always a sucker for a sob story, and apparently Lucy's is worse than most.'

Was it?

Joel leaned his broad shoulders against the wall and looked at his brother thoughtfully.

That would explain a great deal.

Like the sadness in her eyes and the reason she hadn't wanted to give him her details.

He was experienced enough with women to know when someone was attracted to him, and Lucy had been attracted to him.

But she hadn't wanted to be.

Suddenly he was intrigued. 'So what's her story?' He asked the question casually but he didn't feel casual at all. In fact, he felt more serious than he'd felt for a long time.

Maybe ever…

Michael shrugged. 'Don't know. Mum refuses to discuss it. All we know is she's got—'

There was a tap on the door and Ros stuck her head round. 'I've got two urgent calls and Lucy needs someone to see a patient.'

'Add the calls to my list.' Michael stood up.

Joel did the same. He glanced at his father. 'I'll see Lucy's patient.'

Richard frowned. 'Joel…'

'I'm a GP with this practice,' Joel pointed out smoothly. 'I need to start seeing patients some time. It might as well be now.'

Michael shot him a warning glance and Joel smiled.

'Go out and heal the sick, big brother. I promise to behave myself.'

'You better had. Nick and I are watching you. I'll see you later, then.' Michael followed Ros out of the room and Richard caught Joel by the arm to stop him following.

'Joel, I need to talk to you. I know Lucy's pretty, but Nick and Michael are right. She's not your type.' His father's tone was sharp. 'You're to leave her alone.'

Joel looked his father in the eye. 'Where's she living?'

Father looked at son. *'Joel!'*

Joel clapped a hand to his broad chest and looked innocent. 'Did I say a word?'

'You didn't need to. I've known you for thirty-three years and women have always been at the top of your agenda,' his father said dryly. 'Especially pretty ones. Come on, Joel, you're a national heartthrob after that TV series. You're not short of female company and you never have been. You don't need Lucy.'

Oh, yes, he did.

Joel lifted his chin. 'What's the story, Dad?'

His father sighed. 'She doesn't want us to discuss it, so

I'm not going to, but let's just say that there's no way a girl like her is going to want anything to do with a man like you.'

'A man like me?' Joel lifted his eyebrows and glanced down at himself. 'Two legs, two arms, a good pair of shoulders—what's wrong with me?'

'Nothing.' Richard gave a wry smile as he ran his eyes over his son's muscular frame. 'There's nothing at all wrong with you, as you well know.'

'So?'

Richard sighed and shook his head. 'She doesn't want anyone, Joel. And I warn you now, I won't have her pestered. The girl's been through enough.'

What had she been through?

Joel's voice was quiet. 'I'm not in the habit of pestering women, Dad.'

'No, because they usually fall at your feet,' his father agreed, his tone dry. 'But Lucy is different. She came here for a quiet life and that is exactly what she's going to have. She's out of bounds, Joel, and please remember that or your mother will kill me. And she'll kill you too, probably.'

Joel wasn't giving up. 'It was a man, presumably.' His expression was grim as he contemplated the possibilities. 'Did he hit her? Hurt her in some way? Maybe Mike, Nick and I could find the guy—'

His father cut him off with an impatient gesture. 'Put your fists away, Joel. This isn't your battle.' Richard gave a long sigh and rubbed his forehead with the tips of his fingers. 'We all want to help, but she won't accept more than we've done already. I suspect that what she really needs is friendship. She must be very lonely. Your mother and I keep inviting her round but she always refuses.'

'I make a good friend,' Joel said softly, and his father frowned.

'No, Joel! I don't want—'

'Relax, Dad.' Joel put a hand on his father's shoulder, a confident smile playing around his firm mouth. 'You need to learn how to chill out! You're getting too old for all this stress.'

'Too old!' His father choked and spluttered and Joel grinned.

'Trust me, Dad! I'm not going to hurt Lucy. I promise.'

But he'd like to hurt the person who'd done this to her.

His mind still churning over the possibilities, he turned on his heel and sprinted down the stairs before his father had time to warn him off again. One thing was sure: he was going to get to the bottom of what was behind the sadness.

It was the blue-eyed doctor from the accident.

Lucy stopped breathing and stared as he came down the stairs, long limbed and staggeringly handsome.

Oh, no, no, no, no!

Why hadn't it occurred to her before?

The Whittakers all had those same blue eyes, and Richard had told her that his son had worked on the air ambulance, so she really should have guessed.

Joel.

Joel Whittaker.

Why did this have to happen? She loved Richard, and Michael and Nick were both friendly and non-threatening. But as for Joel...

She swallowed hard as she stared into those glittering blue eyes.

Joel was one hundred per cent predatory male and there

was no way she would be able to work with him if he looked at her the way he had this morning.

The way he was looking at her now.

She hadn't thought she'd ever be attracted to a man again and the strength of her reaction to him shocked her.

But she didn't want to feel that way. It just confused her.

'Hello, again.' He paused at the bottom of the stairs and gave her a friendly smile that she had to admit was more boyish than predatory. 'Ros said you needed someone to see a patient?'

She looked at him blankly. It hadn't occurred to her that he'd be starting work straight away.

'Is there someone you're worried about?' he prompted her, and she backed away from him, flustered.

'Yes, but I just wanted to run an idea past someone. It's probably stupid, and I know how busy you all are, and—'

'Lucy.' He interrupted her gently, his eyes searching. 'You can run it past me. I'm a doctor, too, remember?'

As if she needed reminding! His impressive performance at the scene of the accident was still uppermost in her mind. If it hadn't been for him, she dreaded to think what might have happened.

'Can we go into one of the consulting rooms?' She glanced over her shoulder towards her treatment room. 'I don't really want to talk in the corridor.'

He was instantly professional, his blue eyes keenly interested. He strode ahead of her, pushed open Michael's door and stood to one side to let her in.

Closing the door behind them, he stayed with his back to the door, watching her carefully. 'Go on, then—fire away.'

She swallowed. 'Kawasaki disease. Have you ever come across it?'

He nodded slowly. 'Once, when I was doing paeds, but it's pretty rare. Why? Do you think we've got a case?'

Lucy looked at him and started to relax. At least he hadn't laughed or scoffed or tried to tell her that she was overstepping her role.

'I'm probably completely wrong—tell me some more about it. It's not in the textbook I keep in the treatment room.'

Joel took a deep breath and paced across the room to the window. 'Kawasaki disease—otherwise known as mucocutaneous lymph node syndrome—first reported in 1967 in Japan. It's thought to be related to a viral infection and usually affects children under the age of five.' He turned to face her, a frown touching his brow. 'What signs and symptoms does the child have?'

'She's had a temperature for the last five days. She saw Michael once at the beginning, but he thought it was viral, and now she's got a nasty peeling rash on the palms of her hands and the soles of her feet,' Lucy told him. 'And her tongue looks like a strawberry. That's what made me think of it, to be honest. I just remembered the strawberry tongue bit from my training. One of those useless bits of information that stay with you.'

'Clearly not useless,' Joel said softly, walking back across the room and opening the door. 'Michael's gone out on a call so I'll take a look at her with you.'

'They couldn't get an appointment to see one of the doctors today, so she thought she'd ask me about the rash,' Lucy said as they walked to the treatment room. 'I'm probably being ridiculous. It's probably nothing.'

Joel pushed open the door of the treatment room and Lucy introduced him to Millie Gordon and her mother.

Despite the temperature, which was clearly making her feel ill, Millie's eyes widened. 'I thaw you on the television,' she lisped, and Joel grinned at the little girl and squatted down in front of her so that their eyes were on the same level.

'You did?'

She nodded her head. 'My mummy thinkth you're gorgeouth.'

Millie's mother turned a deep shade of pink and Joel threw his head back and laughed, clearly not in the slightest bit embarrassed by Millie's indiscretion.

'Well, that's nice to know.' He was totally confident and relaxed. 'I need all the fans I can get.'

Lucy glanced between them, confused, and then suddenly remembered what the paramedic had said. 'You were on television?'

Mrs Gordon looked at her in surprise. 'You mean you haven't ever seen *Helicopter Doctor*? It's on every Tuesday at seven p.m. It's the most exciting thing on television! We haven't missed a single episode in our house. Even my husband enjoys it. Although not,' she said with a blush, 'for the same reasons as I do. Dr Whittaker is the nation's heartthrob,' she added in an undertone to Lucy.

The nation's heartthrob?

Was he?

It was easy enough to understand. Those gorgeous blue eyes and that killer smile must have had the female viewing public falling to their knees. Combine it with some heroic roadside rescues and he must seem irresistible.

Seemingly indifferent to his growing national reputation, Joel examined the little girl thoroughly, keeping her entertained with stories of life on the air ambulance as he took a good look at her.

'She's had a temperature for five days now and she's very cranky,' Mrs Gordon said softly as Joel checked Millie's mouth and her eyes.

'Any diarrhoea?'

'Some, yes.' Mrs Gordon frowned. 'What do you think it is?'

Joel straightened and crossed his arms across his broad chest. 'It could be a number of things,' he said quietly. 'There's no point in me listing them for you, but Sister Bishop here suspected something called Kawasaki disease and I think she's right. Some people think that it can come on after a viral infection. It may not be that, of course, so it's important that I send her straight to the paediatricians at the hospital so that they can do some tests.'

'Tests?' Mrs Gordon looked shocked. 'What tests?'

'Blood tests mostly,' Joel explained. 'Do you have transport, Mrs Gordon?'

The woman nodded, clearly distracted with worry. 'Yes, I've got the car, but I don't—Is it serious?'

Joel put a hand on her shoulder. 'It can be, but providing we get her into hospital I have every confidence that she'll be fine. I'll ring the paediatrician now so that he'll know to expect you. Sister will help you get Millie to the car while I do a letter.'

Lucy helped Mrs Gordon gather up her things and followed her through to the car park.

'I just wanted you to check the rash.' Mrs Gordon settled Millie onto the booster seat and bit her lip. 'I didn't think—'

'It may be nothing,' Lucy said quietly, 'but better safe than sorry. We'll call the hospital to check how she's doing, and don't be afraid to call us here if there's anything we can do.'

Joel strode across the car park and handed Mrs Gordon a letter. 'Her name is Dr Emma Peterson and she's expecting you. Park in the main car park and take her straight to Kitten Ward, the paediatric unit.'

'Thanks, Dr Whittaker.' Mrs Gordon slid into the driver's seat and reversed carefully out of the space while they watched.

Lucy's expression was troubled. 'Perhaps we should have called them an ambulance.'

'Quicker to drive,' Joel said bluntly, taking her arm and steering her back towards the medical centre. 'Let's get back inside before you catch pneumonia.'

'Do you think it is Kawasaki disease?'

He pulled a face. 'Probably. Could be streptococcal disease or Stevens-Johnson syndrome, but I think you were probably spot on in your diagnosis. I'm impressed.'

She blushed under the warmth of his gaze, wondering how on earth she was going to be able to work with him. The secret was surely just to look on him as a doctor and not a man.

But she'd never met a doctor whose eyes were quite so blue, whose shoulders were quite so broad and whose smile had such a powerful effect on her breathing.

Joel followed Lucy back to the treatment room, unable to let her go so soon.

'I can't believe you thought of Kawasaki,' he said softly, leaning against the door and looking at her. She was obviously as bright as she was beautiful.

And she was very beautiful. His experienced eye could see that she wasn't wearing any make-up, and yet her eyelashes were thick and dark and her skin creamy and smooth.

And as for her mouth...

He had to clench his hands behind his back to stop himself reaching for her.

Aware that he needed to keep it professional if he didn't want to frighten her off, he kept to the subject of work.

'Dad says that you run the asthma clinic and the immunisation clinic,' he said, working hard to keep his tone casual. 'I'm going to be doing those with you, so maybe we ought to meet up some time and you can talk me through how you do things.'

Her eyes widened, reminding him of a startled fawn that had just spotted danger.

'I—I don't think we need to, Dr Whittaker.' The slightly husky tone of her voice curled around his insides and he fought his reaction to her. 'The clinics are fairly standard.'

You didn't need to be a genius to work out that she was trying to spend as little time with him as possible.

'But I haven't worked in general practice before,' he pointed out, telling himself firmly that if he gave in to his instincts and kissed her now, he'd be in serious trouble. 'I really want to get a feel for how you do things.'

She licked her lips in a nervous gesture that almost wrecked him, and he could see from the look in her eyes that she was searching frantically for excuses.

He wondered what it was that she was afraid of.

Was she scared of him physically, or was she afraid of the attraction between them?

Because there *was* an attraction between them and there had been from the moment they'd set eyes on each other at the scene of the accident. But she was obviously determined not to admit it, even to herself.

'To be honest, I'm feeling a bit at sea at the moment,' he lied, suppressing a stab of guilt as he saw the wariness in her eyes turn to concern for him. He was uncomfortably aware that he was taking advantage of her sweet nature but he consoled himself with the fact that he had no intention of hurting her.

'I suppose it must be strange, being in general practice

after the air ambulance,' she said, her husky voice teasing his nerve endings.

He gave her a lopsided smile. 'Dad's giving me some pointers, of course, but I really want to get a feel for the clinics.'

She looked at him and he sensed her reluctance, but suddenly she gave him a fleeting smile.

'All right.'

Joel watched that smile, fascinated by the movement of her mouth and it occurred to him that he couldn't remember when a woman had last been so shy with him.

Was he really that scary?

'How about three o'clock? After your clinic.'

'I can't do that,' she said immediately, her dark hair shining under the lights as she shook her head. 'I finish work at three o'clock.'

He frowned. 'It would only take twenty minutes or so, and—'

'I can't.'

'But—'

'I can't stay late, Dr Whittaker. *Ever.*' She stared him straight in the eye and he held her gaze, his mind working overtime, trying to work out what was going on. His father hadn't mentioned that she worked part time.

Why did she have to leave at three o'clock? He resisted the urge to ask her. He didn't want to push his luck.

'We can meet tomorrow morning,' she suggested finally, 'after your surgery and before you go out on calls.'

'Sounds good to me,' he said casually, carefully concealing all the questions that were running through his mind. 'Tomorrow it is, then.'

He made a mental note to ask his father why Lucy had to leave at three o'clock and then remembered that Michael had been in the middle of saying something when Ros had disturbed them.

What had Michael been about to tell him?

Joel frowned and tried to remember the conversation word for word.

Something about Lucy having…having…

Having what? He frowned and made a mental note to ask Michael over dinner.

'Did you have to have your hair cut quite so short? You look like a hit man.' Elizabeth Whittaker put her hands on her hips, the smile in her eyes belying her words as she frowned up at her youngest son.

'Great to see you too, Mum.' Joel grinned and swept her off her feet into a bear hug. 'And while we're at it, yes, I've still got the motorbike, no, I'm not planning on getting married and, yes, I've brought a ton of washing home. Anything else you want to nag me about while we're at it?'

'Cheeky boy.' Elizabeth stood on tiptoe to kiss his cheek and cast another regretful look at his cropped dark hair. 'You look like a thug. It's no wonder you're not married. I should think most women are terrified of you—'

'As if.' Nick strolled into the room, holding a glass in his hand, closely followed by his wife Tina, who went straight over to Joel's side and gave him a hug.

'Hello, handsome. Good to see you again.'

Nick rolled his eyes and looked at his mother. 'What were you saying about terrified?'

'Joel's not scary, and anyway women secretly love a tough man.' Tina stretched out a hand and ruffled Joel's hair. 'It looks sexy short. Goes with the biceps.'

Joel grinned smugly at his brother. 'You see? One member of the family appreciates me.'

'Just as long as you remember that it is only the one member,' Nick drawled, but the twinkle in his eyes took the sting out of his words.

Joel smiled at Tina. 'So how's the boutique? Still shocking the locals with your daring dresses?'

'Er—yes.' Tina's eyes twinkled and Nick slipped an arm round her.

'She always creates a stir does my Tina. It would help if she remembered that what works in London doesn't always work in deepest Cornwall.'

'Living in Cornwall doesn't mean that we all have to dress in waders all the time,' Tina protested, and Elizabeth raised her voice to make herself heard over the laughter.

'Come on, everyone, dinner's ready.' She waved them all towards the huge conservatory at the back of the house which they used as a dining room. 'Joel, put those biceps to good use and give me a hand to bring things through.'

Joel obediently picked up a tray laden with soup plates and hot crusty rolls, and sniffed appreciatively.

'It's good to be home.'

'It's good to have you.' His mother gave a contented smile. 'I can't believe we've finally lured you back. I thought you might be seduced by your own PR and let yourself be persuaded to start a career in television.'

He'd had offers, and his mother was well aware of it, but she was also aware that he'd never seriously considered any of them.

Joel balanced the tray carefully. 'I love Cornwall, Mum, you know I do. And I love medicine. I was always going to come back. I never intended to stay in London for ever.'

Tina walked across the room and looked at Elizabeth. 'What can I do?'

'Turn the beans down, please; they're boiling their heads off.' Elizabeth quickly checked the meat in the oven and then whipped off her apron. 'Come on, let's eat this soup before it gets cold.'

They settled down at the table and everyone raised their glasses.

'To Joel.'

'The film star.'

Joel grinned and took a slug of his drink. 'Thanks. Not sure about the film-star bit, though.'

They all tucked into their soup and immediately the talk turned to practice business.

'Lucy said that the new fridge has arrived,' Michael told them as he reached for a bread roll, 'so our little problem with vaccines should now be solved.'

'That's good.' Richard glanced across the table to Joel and waved his spoon at him. 'Your first job is to get our immunisation rate up. It's giving me headaches at the moment.'

Joel frowned. 'Are we going to miss our targets?'

'I don't give a damn about the targets,' his father replied. 'I just don't want to see another measles epidemic. You lot are too young to remember just what a serious illness it can be.'

Nick suppressed a yawn. 'It would help if the newspapers would stop printing scare stories.'

Joel looked at them expectantly. 'Any ideas? What have you done so far?'

His father gave a philosophical shrug. 'It's all down to education, of course. But how we get that message out— well, I leave that to you to come up with some suggestions. Lucy's a bright girl—you can see what ideas she has on the subject.'

Michael leaned back in his chair, his eyes alight with humour. 'Maybe he could auction himself. If people complete the full immunisation schedule they're entered into a prize draw for a date with Joel.'

Nick choked on his drink. 'I thought we were planning to increase uptake?'

Tina laughed. 'I think it's a great idea. They'd flock!'

'I was hoping for something a little more conservative,' Richard said mildly, observing his sons with amusement. 'Joel, this is your baby. You and Lucy need to put your heads together.'

Put their heads together?

Now, that was an idea worth pursuing.

Joel's mind ran riot and he had a disturbingly clear vision of sliding his hands into her gorgeous dark hair and lowering his mouth to hers...

He blanked his expression.

Or at least he thought he had.

'Joel!' His mother's voice was unusually sharp. 'I need help with the second course, please.'

Oops.

Obviously his face hadn't been as inscrutable as he'd thought.

Knowing exactly why she wanted him in the kitchen, Joel gave a good-natured grin and followed his mother out of the conservatory.

'You want help with the gravy?' He folded his arms across his broad chest and leaned against the kitchen door, watching while his mother bent down and carefully lifted the meat out of the oven.

'You know why I want you here, Joel.' His mother straightened up, her face flushed. 'And it has nothing to do with the gravy. I've known you for thirty-three years and I can read your mind.'

Joel grinned. 'I sincerely hope not.'

His thoughts about Lucy were definitely something he wasn't prepared to share with his mother.

'Joel.' She put the meat on the kitchen table and looked him straight in the eye. 'I know she's pretty, but I want you to stay away from Lucy.'

'You and the rest of the world, it would seem.' Joel hooked his fingers into the pockets of his trousers and looked at her thoughtfully. 'Everyone seems to be falling over themselves to keep me away from Lucy. Am I such an evil character all of a sudden?'

His mother sighed. 'You know you're not, and I know I shouldn't interfere...'

'Feel free,' Joel said, his tone deceptively mild. 'Everyone else has spent the entire afternoon listing all the reasons why I mustn't corrupt Lucy with my wicked ways. It would be awful if you missed out.'

Elizabeth sensed something in his tone and her face softened. 'Let's get one thing straight here. I don't think you're wicked,' she said quietly, draining the vegetables and tipping them into various bowls. 'But I do think you're totally wrong for Lucy. I know you don't want to settle down, Joel, and that's fine, but Lucy isn't the sort of woman you can seduce and then discard.'

Joel's smile faded. 'I can assure you that I've never "seduced" anyone in my life,' he said coldly. 'All my relationships have been completely mutual.'

Elizabeth looked at her youngest son and gave a lopsided smile. 'Now I've made you angry, and I'm sorry. I didn't mean to overstep the mark. Your trouble is you don't even know your own charm. You break hearts without knowing you're doing it, Joel, and you always have. There's something about you that women can't say no to, and if you—'

'Mum.' Joel lifted a hand and interrupted her, his tone slightly impatient. 'I'm not going to hurt Lucy.'

'But—'

His gaze was steady on hers. 'Trust me, OK?'

Elizabeth stared at him for a long moment and gave a regretful shake of her head. 'You've dated more women than I care to think about, Joel. When are you going to settle down with one of them?'

Joel gave his mother a tired smile. 'Don't let's start on the subject of marriage so early in the evening, hmm? Truth is, I don't believe in mediocre marriages and I've never met anyone that I want to wake up next to every morning for the rest of my life.'

In fact, he was beginning to wonder whether there was something wrong with him. He was used to deflecting his brothers' teasing remarks about his inability to commit, but deep down they rankled.

Why couldn't he find someone he wanted to settle down with?

Was he too choosy?

Did he expect too much?

He breathed out heavily. Well, if he was there was nothing he could do about it. He certainly didn't intend to lower his expectations.

'Let's talk about something else, shall we?'

His mother looked at him guiltily. 'You're telling me I'm out of line.'

'Yes, but I'm trying to do it nicely.' He gave her a gentle smile and picked up a pile of plates. 'I tolerate your interference because you're my mother and I adore you. I let you go further than most, but I still have limits.'

Elizabeth picked up the meat and followed him across the kitchen. 'Just as long as you promise to leave Lucy alone.'

Joel stopped dead and looked at his mother with a steady gaze. 'I can't do that.'

No way would he make a promise he knew he couldn't keep.

His mother stared at him in exasperation. 'But—'

'I promised not to hurt her, and I won't,' Joel said, his soft tone a warning to her to stop interfering. 'Now, change the subject Mum.'

It was only when dinner was over and he was back in his penthouse apartment overlooking the harbour that he suddenly remembered he'd forgotten to ask Michael about Lucy.

He still didn't know why she needed to leave work at three o'clock.

CHAPTER THREE

ON THE way to work the next morning, Lucy called in to see Ivy Williams.

'I was wondering how you were,' she said quietly, moving past the old lady into the hallway and waiting while she shut the door. Despite the freezing weather, Ivy's house was warm and snug and she was clearly looking after herself.

'Well, it's hard,' Ivy confessed, her face lined and tired. 'Did you know that we'd only been together for ten years?'

Lucy shook her head. 'No. No, I didn't know that.'

'When you lose a partner in your seventies, people assume that you've been together for ever, but it wasn't like that for Bert and me,' Ivy told her quietly. 'I was married to someone else before Bert, you know. And I suppose I was happy enough. At least, I thought I was. I never knew any differently until he died. Then I met Bert and I realised what I'd been missing for all those years. What I had with Bert was—' She broke off, her eyes glistening with unshed tears. 'Well, let's just say it was the fairy tale. And you don't imagine that you're going to find that when you're sixty.'

Lucy bit her lip and felt a lump building in her throat. 'It must be so hard for you. And you didn't have that long together.'

Ivy gave a wistful smile. 'I would rather have lived one day with a man I truly loved than a lifetime in a lesser relationship. And we had ten years together.' Ivy sniffed and made a visible effort to pull herself together. 'Some people go through life and never know what true love and passion is. At least I wasn't one of those. But it's hard, being without him. I see him everywhere. In the garden, in the living room...'

Lucy slipped an arm around her shoulders. 'Has your daughter been to see you?'

'Oh, yes, she's very good.' Ivy sighed and managed a smile. 'She wants me to go and live with them.'

'And will you?'

'I don't know,' Ivy said slowly. 'Maybe. I'm not sure. They have young children, so I can't believe they'd really want me there. And I'm not sure if I want to leave the house. The memories are everywhere, and it hurts, but I'm not sure that I want to be without it.'

Lucy nodded. 'Well, don't make any sudden decisions.'

'No.' Ivy shook her head and looked at Lucy. 'You're a kind girl, coming to visit an old thing like me when I know you're busy.'

'I'm not busy,' Lucy lied, 'and I was going to come yesterday but I was caught up helping with an accident on the coast road.'

'I can imagine that the roads are lethal at the moment,' Ivy observed. 'Was anyone hurt?'

Lucy gave a little shudder as she remembered the events of the day before.

'A motorcyclist, but hopefully he'll be all right. Dr Whittaker's youngest son happened to be passing, fortunately, so he was well cared for.'

'Young Joel?' Ivy's face softened. 'He's a lad, that one. More girlfriends than I've had hot dinners, and no sign of settling down with any of them. He gives his mother grey hairs. But he's a nice boy.'

Boy?

There was nothing boyish about Joel Whittaker, Lucy

reflected ruefully when she finally picked her way along the icy pavement to her car.

He was all man. Every handsome inch of him.

And it came as no surprise to learn that he was lousy at commitment. In her limited experience, all men were.

She made her way back to the surgery and was soon involved with her patients, checking blood pressures, taking bloods and offering a variety of health-related advice.

It was early afternoon and Lucy had just finished syringing an old lady's ear when Joel tapped on her door and strolled in.

'I just called the hospital about Millie Gordon. Your diagnosis was spot on. Kawasaki disease. Frankly, I'm impressed.'

'Oh.' Lucy blushed, flustered by the look of admiration in his blue eyes.

He was a doctor, she reminded herself firmly. No different from Nick or Michael.

Which was utter nonsense, of course. Joel was about as different as it was possible to be.

Since she'd met him she hadn't been able to get him out of her mind, and the effect he was having on her worried and puzzled her. Today he was wearing a pair of dark, well-cut trousers and a midnight-blue roll-neck jumper which brushed his dark jawline.

Was it just because he was so good-looking?

Millie's mother had said that he was the nation's heartthrob. Was she just suffering from a normal female reaction?

Lucy licked her lips and tried to keep her mind on work. 'So is she very poorly?'

Joel dropped into one of her chairs and hooked his thumbs in the pockets of his trousers. 'I spoke to the paediatric registrar and she said that Millie's doing OK, considering. It was lucky that she asked to see you rather than wait for an appointment with one of us doctors.' He breathed out heavily. 'If she hadn't done that and there'd been a delay...'

'Well, there wasn't,' Lucy pointed out, and Joel nodded.

'At the next practice meeting we need to talk about this case.' Joel was clearly worried about it. 'If she'd gone home and waited for the next available appointment then it would have been a different story. We caught it early because of you.'

'All the doctors here are good about seeing children, no matter how busy they are,' Lucy informed him quietly. 'If she'd insisted, she would have been slotted in. She didn't insist because she'd seen Michael a few days before.'

Joel nodded. 'And he didn't do anything wrong. In the beginning there's nothing to distinguish it from any other viral illness. According to the notes, he asked her to come back in forty-eight hours if the temperature hadn't come down or if she was worried.'

'But she didn't want to bother him,' Lucy said softly. 'It's a common problem, don't you find? The patients that really need to see you never like to insist.'

'Whereas the ones that could very well survive without seeing a doctor virtually live here,' Joel agreed, getting to his feet and pacing across her room to look out of the window. 'Well, anyway, I've told Michael all about it because technically Millie is his patient. She's obviously going to be in hospital for a while yet.'

Lucy nodded. 'I hope she's going to be all right.'

'Me, too.'

'I asked after our motorcyclist as well, by the way.'

'And?' Lucy's heart beat slightly faster as she thought back to yesterday afternoon. 'Is he going to survive?'

Joel nodded. 'He needed a massive transfusion and a long time in theatre, but he's definitely off the critical list.'

'Well, that's a relief,' Lucy breathed. 'I never, ever want to be the first person at the scene of an accident again.'

'You did everything right.'

She waited for him to say something else but he didn't. Instead, he just looked at her, his eyes very blue, and her heart suddenly started to beat faster.

What was it that happened to her when he was in the room?

She didn't understand it. All she knew was that it was something she didn't want.

She sensed that he was about to speak when the door opened and Ros entered.

'Have you got time to see two extras, Lucy? Oh, sorry, Dr Whittaker...' She paused in the doorway, her expression apologetic. 'I didn't realise you were in here.'

'I was just leaving,' Joel said softly, his gaze lingering on Lucy for a long moment before he strolled towards the door.

Lucy was sure that Ros would notice her tell-tale blush, but the older woman didn't seem to, chatting instead about the old lady who'd tripped on the kerb and needed a dressing on her leg.

'I'll do it right away, Ros.' Lucy cleared her throat and delved in her cupboard for a dressing pack, relieved that Joel had left the room. Without his presence to unnerve her she felt back in control again.

What had he been about to say?

And why, when a new relationship was the last thing she wanted, did she react so strongly to him?

Because he was so good-looking, she reasoned as she prepared to dress the leg. He was an incredibly handsome man—any woman would look twice at him. Even a woman like her, whose life was in tatters.

Comforted by the thought that her feelings were completely normal, Lucy threw her attention into work and the afternoon flew past.

She took advantage of a brief lull mid-afternoon to finish stacking the boxes of vaccine into the new fridge. She'd virtually finished when Ros bustled into the room.

'Lucy, I need you to—' She broke off and stared at the fridge. 'Oh, you're doing the fridge! I can't believe it's finally arrived after all that fuss!'

Lucy smiled and closed the door firmly. 'Yes, it's about time, isn't it?' She scrambled to her feet. 'You said you needed me?'

Ros pulled a face. 'I've got a girl crying in Reception. A very young girl. Wants to see a lady doctor. Of course we don't have a lady doctor. Only four hulking males—totally useless at a time like this.'

Lucy gave a smile of understanding. 'I'll see her and decide whether she needs to see someone.'

Ros sighed with relief. 'You're a star. I'll send her through. Her name is Penny, by the way, and more than that she will not tell me, poor lass.'

Penny walked hesitantly into the room, her face pale and blotched with crying. Lucy's heart went out to her. She'd never seen a more miserable-looking creature.

'Penny?' She closed the door behind Ros and guided the girl to a chair. 'Sit down and tell me what's upsetting you.'

'I've been so stupid.' The girl's face crumpled and she started to cry again, great tearing sobs that shook her whole body.

'Oh, Penny!' Touched by the girl's distress, Lucy instinctively slipped an arm around her shoulders and held the girl tightly until the sobs lessened. 'Tell me what's happened.'

Penny gave an enormous sniff and wiped her nose on the sleeve of her coat. 'You're going to think I'm so silly...'

'I would never think that,' Lucy assured her quickly.

Penny gave a sniff. 'I just didn't know who to turn to.'

'Well, you can start with me,' Lucy said quietly. 'Sometimes when you have a problem it's easier to talk to people that you don't know very well.'

She sank back onto her heels, her arm still on Penny's shoulder.

'Do you promise not to tell my mum?'

A quick glance at the notes showed her that the girl was seventeen. Lucy bit her lip, knowing that she had to be careful what she said. 'What happens here is confidential, just between you and I. But you're very young, Penny. You shouldn't be shouldering big problems on your own. I'm sure your Mum would want to know if something was upsetting you this badly. Tell me what's happened, sweetheart, and we'll work out what to do together.'

Penny took a deep breath. 'I slept with a boy last night and now I wish I hadn't.' Having blurted it out, Penny started to cry again and Lucy handed her a box of tissues.

'Why do you wish you hadn't?'

'Because now I might be pregnant,' Penny choked, and Lucy's voice was gentle.

'You didn't use any contraception?'

Penny shook her head, her breath coming out in jerks as she spoke. 'No. I didn't think of it, and neither did he. And what if I've caught something awful?'

'Take a deep breath for me, Penny.' Lucy tried to soothe her, handing her a box of tissues. 'That's right. Now, then, let's take this one step at a time. This happened last night, you say?'

Penny nodded.

'So we need to give you some emergency contraception.'

'But I thought you could only take it the morning after. And it's the afternoon now so it's too late.'

'You can take it up to seventy-two hours after you've had sex,' Lucy told her, 'so it certainly isn't too late.'

'I don't know why I did it.' Penny shook her head slowly and looked at Lucy helplessly. 'I met him at a party and I wasn't even meant to be there. I told Mum I was sleeping over at a friend's. He was gorgeous—older, really good-looking. I suppose I got carried away.'

Lucy gave her a sympathetic smile. 'It happens.'

'Well, I wish it hadn't,' Penny whispered, shredding the tissue with her fingers. 'I'm in a complete panic now. I know I need to see a doctor, but Mum has known Dr Richard since they were at school together and he'll tell her.'

Lucy frowned. 'You're seventeen, Penny, and what happens between a doctor and a patient is confidential. I can assure you that Dr Whittaker wouldn't tell your mother.'

Penny pulled a face. 'It isn't just that. Even if I knew he wasn't going to tell Mum, I still couldn't talk to him— he'd never understand. It's a generation thing, isn't it? I don't suppose he's had sex for years. It would be too embarrassing.'

Lucy wondered what Richard's reaction would be if he could hear the conversation. 'Well, if it's age that's worrying you, how about seeing Dr Michael?'

Penny hesitated and then nodded. 'Yes. All right. I expect he does at least know what sex is.'

Completely sure that Richard Whittaker also knew all

too well what sex was, Lucy smothered a smile as she left the room and slipped along the corridor to Michael's room.

She tapped on the door and opened it, but it wasn't Michael who was sitting there, it was Joel.

'Oh.' Lucy stopped dead, taken aback to see him, and then mumbled an apology and went to leave the room.

'Hold on.' His deep voice stopped her in her tracks and he stood up and walked round the desk towards her. 'Did you want something?'

'No.' She certainly didn't. At least, not from him. *He unsettled her more than any man she'd ever met.* 'I mean, yes. Michael. I was looking for Michael to see a patient.'

His gaze was disconcertingly sharp. 'He's gone on a house call. I'm covering his surgery. What can I do for you?'

In the confines of the consulting room his shoulders seemed broader than ever and the dark jumper he was wearing just emphasised the blue of his eyes.

He looked wickedly handsome and she swallowed hard and fumbled behind her for the doorhandle.

'Nothing. It doesn't matter.'

'Now you've intrigued me.' He gave a curious smile and rested one muscular thigh on the desk. 'What is it that Michael has that I don't?'

She bit her lip and rubbed her damp palms on her uniform. 'Nothing. It's not you. I mean—well...' she was fumbling in her confusion. 'It's just that I need someone sympathetic.'

One dark eyebrow lifted and humour flickered in those blue eyes. 'You don't think I'm sympathetic?'

Hideously aware that she'd just insulted him, she blushed with mortification. 'Of course you are—I didn't mean... It's just that I need someone...older.'

Oh, help, she was talking total gibberish. But she just didn't think Joel was the right person for Penny.

'Older.' He nodded slowly and folded his arms across his broad chest. 'Now I really *am* intrigued. Why don't you tell me the problem and then we'll work out whether I'm old enough to deal with it?'

Relieved that he was still laughing, and didn't seem annoyed by her tactless comments, Lucy briefly told him what had happened and the humour faded from his eyes.

'Ouch,' he said softly. 'Poor kid. She must be terrified.'

'She is.'

'Who's she registered with?'

'Your father, but she doesn't want to see him because he's a family friend and because…'

'Because?' he prompted her gently, and she blushed.

'Because she thinks he's too old to understand about sex.'

Joel threw back his head and laughed, his eyes shimmering with delight. 'Oh, that's fantastic. We're always pulling his leg about being old. I must remember that one!'

Lucy looked at him anxiously. 'You mustn't tell him.'

'Don't worry, I won't disclose the source.' Joel's shoulders were still shaking. 'OK, so what are we going to do about young Penny?' His laughter fading, he stood up in a smooth movement, his eyes on her face. 'Seeing as all the other Whittakers are occupied elsewhere, are you going to trust me with her?'

Lucy hesitated, not sure what Penny's reaction would be to talking to Joel. She was certain that if it was her, she'd never be able to discuss sex with a man like him.

Just thinking of Joel and sex made her feel strange.

'Ideally she wants to see a woman.'

He gave a soft laugh and rubbed a hand over his roughened jaw line. 'Well, I'm certainly not a woman, but I promise to be sensitive if that's what's worrying you.'

Lucy felt her breathing quicken as their eyes locked. 'All right.'

To her relief, Penny seemed delighted to see Joel.

'You're that doctor from the television.'

Lucy decided that she must be the only person on the planet that hadn't seen the *Helicopter Doctor* series. She made a mental note to try and see it one night.

Joel chatted with Penny for a few minutes, helping her to relax, and then he smoothly switched into professional mode and talked through what had happened.

Lucy stood to one side, listening while he questioned the girl and talked quietly about the dangers of unprotected sex.

She had to hand it to him, he was good. He talked at exactly the right level, never patronising her but always making sure that the information he gave was well within the limits of Penny's understanding. He covered everything and told her exactly what she needed to do next.

And Penny seemed to calm down as she talked to him.

'Are you going to tell Mum?'

'No.' Joel's voice was calm. 'But you might want to think about telling her yourself. She might be more understanding than you think.'

He talked to her about contraception for the future, checked her blood pressure and other risk factors, then prescribed emergency contraception.

When Penny finally left the surgery she was looking a lot happier.

Lucy gave Joel a hesitant smile. 'Thanks for seeing her. Do you think she'll take your advice and go to the sexual health clinic?'

'I doubt it.' He gave a resigned shrug and then his eyes gleamed. 'Did I pass?'

'Pass?' She looked at him, confused, and he grinned.

'Was I sensitive enough?'

He'd been brilliant, but she wasn't going to tell him that.

'You were—' Suddenly she caught sight of the clock and gasped in horror. It was already five past three. 'Oh, my God. I've got to go.'

He lifted an eyebrow and looked at her quizzically. 'What's the hurry? I thought we were going to have a chat about those clinics. We didn't seem to find time this morning.'

'I know, and I'm sorry. But it's already past three o'clock.' She grabbed her coat and reached for her car keys, knowing that she didn't have any time to spare. As it was, if she hit traffic she'd be in trouble. 'Maybe tomorrow.'

He planted himself between her and the door. 'Don't keep running away from me, Lucy.' His soft voice played havoc with her nerve endings. 'I'm not going to hurt you. You can trust me.'

Trust him?

She didn't trust anyone.

'It's gone three o'clock,' she croaked, avoiding his eyes. 'If you'll excuse me, I have to go.'

She was already late.

He must have seen the panic in her eyes because he moved to one side and his voice was surprisingly gentle. 'What's so important that you have to run off at three o'clock? Is something wrong? Is there anything I can do?'

His concern affected her more than she'd imagined possible.

'No.'

There was nothing anybody could do.

'Lucy…'

She knew she had to get away from him before she started crying on his very broad shoulders.

As it was, she was going to have to drive like the devil to make it on time.

And she had to be on time.

Being late just wasn't an option.

She slipped past him and sprinted towards the car park, her breath coming in jerks as panic started to swamp her.

Dear God, she was going to be late. She should never have seen that extra patient for Ros. But even as she thought it she knew that she'd have done the same thing again—how could she have left someone as upset as Penny? And if she had turned her away, would Penny have gone elsewhere for her contraception or would she just have left it? Shuddering at what that might have meant, Lucy fumbled with her keys, dropping them in her haste to open the car.

She should have kept a closer watch on the time. She should have asked someone else to chaperone Joel while he examined Penny.

But she'd built up a relationship with the girl.

Frustrated by the choices she was forced to make, she dragged the car door open, slid into the driver's seat and jammed the key into the ignition.

Nothing happened.

Nothing at all.

The engine was dead.

'No!' She sobbed with frustration and panic flooded over her as she turned the key again.

The car was totally dead.

'No, don't do this to me! Not now.'

Her door was suddenly jerked open and Joel stuck his head in. 'What's up?'

'My car's dead.' she turned the key again, her fingers shaking and her heart pounding frantically. 'What am I going to do? I can't be late. I just can't. I need to get a taxi.' She scrambled out of the car and tried to push Joel out of the way, but it was like trying to move a brick wall. He was six feet two of solid muscle.

'Open the bonnet and I'll take a look at it for you,' he suggested calmly, and she thumped a fist against his chest to try and move him.

'You just don't get it, do you?' Her eyes blazed into his, panic making her uncharacteristically impatient. 'You have no idea what happens if I'm late.' She gulped and tried to calm herself down. 'I've tried so hard not to let this happen.'

'Late where? Let what happen?' Joel caught her shoulders in his strong hands and forced her to look at him. 'Where are you going? Lucy—tell me what's wrong and I'll help you.'

He didn't know where she was going?

Hadn't anyone told him?

'You want to help me?' Her breath was coming in jerks. 'If you really want to help, Dr Whittaker, you can call me a taxi. I need to get to the school to pick up my son.'

CHAPTER FOUR

HER SON?

Joel steered Michael's car skillfully down the side roads, taking advantage of his local knowledge to get to Harbour First School as fast as possible.

He should have guessed.

What with his whole family being so protective.

He should have guessed Lucy had a child. That was obviously what Michael had been about to tell him when Ros had disturbed them.

The minute she'd made that announcement he'd sprinted back to the Health Centre, bumping into Michael who had just returned from his house call. Without pausing to give an explanation, Joel had relieved him of his car keys and had bundled a shaking Lucy into the passenger seat.

He still didn't understand why she was so panicky about being a few minutes late, but her utter desperation affected him in a way he hadn't experienced before and he knew he had to help her.

Now she sat next to him in frozen stillness, her eyes fixed on the road ahead.

Instinctively he reached out a hand to grasp hers and felt a rush of satisfaction when she didn't pull away.

'A whole year,' she whispered, her fingers shaking slightly under his. 'For a whole year I've made sure that this never happened. That I was never, ever late. And now…'

She gulped and swallowed and he tightened his grip.

'Calm down.' His voice was strong and solid. 'We're nearly there. You're only five minutes late.'

She snatched her hand away from him and turned to look at him, tears shimmering in her amazing green eyes. 'You don't understand.'

Well, that was true.

But he intended to get to the bottom of it as soon as possible, he thought grimly as he pulled up outside the school and jerked on the handbrake.

She was out of the car before he'd switched off the engine, her shiny dark hair flying around her shoulders as she raced across the playground to the front door of the school.

Joel was hot on her heels.

The door opened and he recognised the headmistress, Isobel Hawker. She'd been headmistress of the First School for as long as anyone could remember, and she was his father's patient.

Her expression was concerned as she looked at Lucy. 'Mrs Bishop—'

'I'm so sorry.' Lucy looked at her with trepidation and the headmistress sighed.

'He's in the classroom, but he's—'

'I can imagine how he is.' Not waiting around for a discussion, Lucy sped off in the direction of the classroom, and Joel followed her, barely pausing to greet Mrs Hawker.

Lucy stopped dead in the doorway of the classroom. There was just one child left in the room and Joel saw her eyes glisten with tears as she stared at the boy.

He was sitting on a pile of cushions, his face pale and swollen from crying, his little shoulders slumped with exhaustion. The class teacher was stroking his back gently and she looked up with an expression of relief when she saw Lucy.

'Sam, here's Mummy now! There, I told you she'd come.'

Sam lifted his head and his face crumpled.

'Oh, sweetheart…' Lucy ran across the room and dropped to her knees, gathering his shaking body against her chest and holding him tightly.

Joel felt his throat close.

Damn.

What was going on?

Why the hell was the child so upset?

'I thought—I thought…' The words came out in between sobs and Lucy tightened her grip on the child.

'I know what you thought,' she whispered, stroking Sam's hair gently with her free hand. 'And I'm so, so sorry I'm late.'

'You promised you'd never be late.'

Lucy squeezed her eyes tightly shut and Joel could almost feel her guilt. 'I know I did, but—'

'You said nothing would ever make you late.' Sam lifted his head to look at her, and even across the room Joel read the accusation in his eyes.

'I know that, sweetheart, but my car wouldn't start.'

Unable to bear the stricken look on Lucy's face any longer, Joel stepped forward, squatting down next to them so that his eyes were level with Sam's.

He didn't know what the hell he was going to say, but he knew he had to say something.

'Hi, there, Sam, I'm Joel.' He cleared his throat and paused. What he knew about little boys could be written on a postage stamp. Unless they were sick, of course. But he remembered reading somewhere that you should always be honest with children, and he took a deep breath. 'It wasn't your mum's fault. She couldn't help being late. When the weather is cold, like it is at the moment, sometimes cars just don't start. I'm going to take a look at your mummy's car and see if I can mend it so that this doesn't happen again.'

Sam stared at him for a moment, his face still pale, then he turned back to Lucy. 'It wouldn't start?'

'That's right.' Lucy nodded and Joel could see just how hard she was struggling not to give way to tears. She took a deep breath. 'We need to go home, sweetheart, and we can talk more, later.'

The little boy was trembling now. 'I thought you weren't coming. I thought I'd been bad and you didn't want me any more...'

Joel felt as though something heavy had landed in the middle of his chest.

Why would any child think a thing like that?

Lucy took another deep breath and caught the little boy by the shoulders, forcing him to look at her. 'Sam, I want you to listen to me, because there's something you need to understand.' Despite the dampness of her dark lashes, her voice was firm and steady as she talked to her child. 'There is nothing, *nothing*, you could do that would stop me wanting you.'

'But Dad...'

Lucy's face lost all its colour and her eyes were tortured. 'We're not talking about your dad, Sam,' she said, her voice shaking slightly as she spoke. 'We're talking about me. I know I was late today, but you should have known I would come. *I always come.*'

Joel felt an unfamiliar feeling in the back of his throat and wondered what on earth was happening to him. Offhand he couldn't remember a single occasion in his adult life when he'd felt like crying and here he was ready to bawl his eyes out over the anguish of a little boy he didn't even know.

What the hell had the guy done to them?

Lucy lifted her head and looked at him, her arms still wrapped tightly around her child. 'I need to get him home. Will—would you be able to give us a lift? I know I shouldn't ask. You've done so much already.' Her cheeks coloured slightly and she stammered slightly as she spoke, clearly embarrassed to be asking favours. 'M-maybe I c-could call a taxi.'

A taxi?

Over his dead body.

'I'll give you a lift. It's no problem, Lucy.'

He had no intention of letting them out of his sight. Not until both of them were smiling again.

He stood up and ran a hand over his jaw, stunned by his own reaction to her plight. Over the years he'd thought he'd experienced every emotion it was possible to feel for the opposite sex—*except love, of course*—but he'd never felt this overwhelming need to take care of a woman before.

Until now.

But with Lucy looking up at him with those huge green eyes, he suddenly understood why his brothers had been so ridiculously protective of her. There was something about her. A gentleness—*a vulnerability*—that made you want to hunt for a dragon just so that you could slay it.

She scrambled to her feet and scooped Sam into her arms. Joel could see that there was no way she was going to let the boy go so he didn't offer to help.

He waited while she spoke to the teacher in a low voice and then followed close behind her as she walked back through the school and out to the car.

Lucy sat with Sam on the back seat of the car, tormented with worry about what had happened and how pale he was.

How could she have put him through that?

For a whole year she'd been so careful, and now…

Would it all happen again? The nightmares, the bed-wetting—just when she'd thought things were improving.

She reached for Sam's hand and then she heard the wheeze.

Oh, dear God, not that. Not now.

'Try and calm down, Sam,' she said, her voice shaking slightly as she soothed him. 'I'm just going to give you your puffer.'

'What's the problem?' Joel glanced into the rear-view mirror, his sharp eyes immediately taking in the situation as he looked at the boy. 'He's asthmatic?'

'Yes.' Lucy rummaged frantically in her bag for his inhaler, digging through loose pieces of paper, her purse, a hairbrush and assorted toys that had crept inside. 'I can't believe I've done this to him.'

'I'll pull over.'

Joel stopped the car, released his seat belt and twisted round so that he could take a look at the child.

Finally Lucy found the puffer buried deep in her bag and handed it to Sam with shaking hands.

'I'm OK, Mum,' the little boy mumbled, and Lucy was aware that Joel was watching the child carefully, counting his respirations and trying to judge just how serious it was.

'We'll get him back to the flat and check his peak flow,' he said quietly, and she nodded, relieved that Joel was there.

It had only taken a short acquaintance for her to realise what an exceptionally talented doctor he was. If Sam needed help then she was confident that Joel could give it.

'Is he coming, too?' Sam looked at Joel suspiciously as he started the engine again.

'Dr Whittaker is going to give us a lift home and then

check your breathing,' Lucy explained, leaning forward to give Joel directions to her flat.

'I know where you live,' he said quietly, and in no time at all they arrived at the new development that had been built near the harbour.

Lucy stepped out of the car and looked at him gratefully. 'Thank you.'

She didn't dare think about what would have happened if he hadn't helped her.

'Let's get him upstairs.'

She bit her lip, knowing that she shouldn't be leaning on this man.

She didn't want to lean on anyone ever again.

'I—'

He must have read her mind because suddenly his eyes were very gentle. 'I'm a doctor, remember? I'll check him over for you and then I'll leave you in peace, OK?'

She nodded slowly, knowing that she couldn't refuse. Knowing that she wouldn't rest unless he'd taken a look at Sam for her. Since she'd arrived in Cornwall she hadn't even had time to register with a GP. She'd thought Sam's asthma was pretty much under control, but after today...

Joel locked the car and strode with her towards the entrance of the apartments.

'I was forgetting that you know your way round here,' she said, following him to the lift. 'But your parents own it, so of course you do.'

'And it so happens that I live on the top floor,' he said quietly, reaching out a hand to press the button.

He lived here?

Just one floor above her?

She glanced at him, startled, but there was nothing threatening about his expression, just a kindness and a strength that unsettled her even more.

'This is you, I believe.' He held the lift door open and she dug in her coat pocket for the keys to her flat.

Every time she opened the door she counted her blessings.

The flat was beautiful.

Light and airy with fabulous views over the harbour and polished wooden floors.

Just being there made her feel better.

'Do you have a peak-flow meter?' Joel was cool and professional as he gave Sam a thorough check. 'What's his normal peak flow? Do you have a chart?'

She nodded and hurried through to the bedroom, returning with the chart in her hand. She waited while he examined Sam and then handed him the chart.

'He seems OK.' Joel reassured her quietly. 'But if he gets any worse you can nip up one floor and bang on my door. I'll be happy to see him for you any time.'

His blue gaze was disturbingly intense and she shifted.

'Thank you,' she said breathlessly. 'Thank you for the lift and for checking him for me.'

'My pleasure.' His eyes held hers for another moment and then he made for the door, glancing casually over his shoulder as he went. 'Bye, Sam.'

There was a pause while Sam stared at him. 'Bye.'

Lucy watched the door close behind Joel and pushed away the feeling of desolation that wrapped itself around her as he disappeared.

Bearing the responsibility of an ill child alone was a responsibility that she found awesome, and it had been soothing to have Joel's reassuring presence. Now that he'd gone she felt more alone than ever.

Pulling herself together, she concentrated her attention on Sam, talking to him about what had happened, satisfying herself that he understood that she would always be there. Apart from keeping a constant eye on where she was, he seemed to have recovered well and wasn't nearly as upset as she'd first feared.

Maybe he was starting to recover.

'You came,' he mumbled sleepily as she snuggled him under the duvet that night.

'I'll always come,' she replied simply, bending to kiss him before turning on the little night-light he insisted on. 'And I'll always love you.'

She pulled his door behind her as she left the room, leaving it open a chink so that she could check on him.

Joel rang the bell and waited, staring at the door of Lucy's flat.

What the hell was he doing?

He'd promised himself that he'd stay away from her, and here he was standing outside her door like a panting, hormonal teenager.

Damn, he was losing it.

And she obviously hadn't heard the doorbell.

Maybe she'd already gone to bed. It was only half past eight but she'd looked exhausted after all the trauma of the afternoon.

He thrust his hands in his pockets to stop himself reaching for the bell a second time, and was just turning away when the door opened.

Lucy stood there, clearly startled to see him. 'Dr Whittaker, what—?'

He said the first thing that came into his head. 'I came to borrow some sugar.'

Her eyes widened. 'Sugar?'

'Yes.' He rummaged in his head for something reasonable to say. 'I need...sugar.'

He could tell by the look in her eyes that she wasn't fooled.

'So where's the bowl?'

He stared at her. 'What bowl?'

For a moment he thought he saw the glimmer of a smile touch her full mouth. 'The bowl for the sugar, Dr Whittaker.'

'Oh…' He stared down at his hands and then gave a helpless smile. 'I'm a hopeless liar.'

'Don't berate yourself for that,' she said quietly, a sad smile touching her eyes. 'Being able to lie convincingly is not top of the list of qualities I most admire in a man.'

She was obviously referring to Sam's father and Joel felt his guts tighten as they always did when he thought about what had happened to her.

'Look…' His smile faded and he treated himself to a long look into her amazing green eyes. 'The truth is, I don't know what I'm doing here. I shouldn't be here, I know that.'

He gave a sigh and closed his eyes briefly. When he opened them she was staring at him, her gaze clear and direct.

'So why are you?'

'Because I needed to see you. I wanted to know that you and Sam were all right.'

Her smile did strange things to his insides. 'That's kind of you. He's asleep.'

'That's good.' He stood awkwardly in the doorway, reminding himself that she was a single mother with a child. He didn't mess around with single mothers. Especially not one as gentle and vulnerable as Lucy. His family were right. She really wasn't his type. 'And how are you?'

'Fine,' she said, but one look at the dark shadows under her eyes told him that she was lying.

'Have you had supper?' He couldn't believe he'd just asked her that question. It was as if his brain and his hormones were operating separately. Get away from her, Whittaker! Leave the girl alone. 'I'm a good cook.'

She looked at him warily. 'I—I'm not hungry.'

'You've got to eat,' he said gruffly, frowning as he saw how tired she looked. 'Give me five minutes to scoop some stuff up from my kitchen and I'll be down to cook you something.'

Her gorgeous full mouth moved into a slight smile. 'Surely you have more exciting things to do with your evening than play chef for me, Dr Whittaker?'

'I'm at a loose end,' he lied. 'So—do you eat pasta?'

Her head tilted to one side, and he knew instantly that she was looking for an ulterior motive for his proposal.

'Just pasta,' he said quickly, placing a hand in the middle of his chest and giving her a reassuring smile. 'No funny business. Scout's honour.'

She laughed. A lovely, bubbly sound that made him want to laugh, too. 'You're too big to be a Scout.' She watched him for a moment, her smile fading slowly. 'Why on earth would you want to cook me pasta, Dr Whittaker?'

'I want to show off my culinary skills,' he said, flexing his muscles and giving her a wink. 'Trust me. You'll be impressed. My mother taught me.'

She was still laughing, but he could see that she was hesitating.

He took advantage of her indecision. 'Go on,' he pushed, 'I'm offering to put a meal in front of you.'

'All right,' she said finally, her eyes slightly shy, and he grinned.

'You won't regret it. Give me five minutes to raid my fridge...'

He sprinted up the stairs to his penthouse before she

could change her mind, loaded the ingredients into a bag, added a bottle of wine and then made his way back to her flat.

He tapped gently on her door and she opened it almost immediately. She'd changed out of her uniform into a pair of faded jeans, and her dark hair flowed loose over her fluffy cream jumper.

Trying valiantly to ignore the way her jeans clung to her long legs, Joel followed her through to the kitchen.

'OK.' He rolled up his sleeves and washed his hands. 'Do you mind breathing garlic over everyone tomorrow?'

She laughed. 'You tell me. You're the one I'll be breathing on.'

'I don't mind.' He peeled a few cloves and chopped them. 'We need to ward off the germs at this time of year. So, Sam went to sleep with no problems?'

She nodded. 'Yes, surprisingly. I was expecting problems but he seems to be all right.'

Joel tossed garlic, olives and baby tomatoes into a pan of sizzling olive oil and cast her a searching look.

'Are you going to tell me what that was all about?' His voice was soft. 'Why can't you ever be late picking Sam up, Lucy? Why was he so upset?'

Suddenly he remembered his father saying that she didn't talk about her past and he cursed his curiosity.

'Look, forget I asked,' he said gruffly. 'It's none of my business.'

She looked at him and gave a wan smile. 'It's all right. You have every right to ask. If it hadn't been for your help today I would have been even later picking him up.' She took a deep breath and her eyes were clouded with painful memories. 'Sam's father decided that he didn't want to be with us any more and so he left.' Her tone was matter-of-fact. 'Unfortunately, he didn't bother to tell us. He just left a note and vanished.'

Joel turned the heat off under the sauce and put down the spoon he'd been using to stir the pan. 'He didn't tell you he was leaving?'

He looked at her in disbelief and she shook her head slowly.

'No, he didn't tell anyone.' She bit her lip. 'And the day he chose to leave he was due to pick Sam up from school. I'd gone to stay with my mother for the night, because she wasn't well, but I hadn't bothered telling the school because I assumed Tim was picking Sam up.'

'Oh, my God.' Joel closed his eyes briefly and when he opened them again she was perched on the edge of the kitchen table, staring at the floor. 'So no one turned up to collect him?'

She shook her head. 'The school rang round everyone in the class and one of the mothers remembered me mentioning that I was going away, but she didn't know where my mother lived. They tried to get hold of Tim, but of course he'd gone.' She gave a little shudder. 'In the end Sam spent the night with a schoolfriend and the next day, when I arrived home, I found Tim's note and guessed what must have happened.'

'No wonder Sam was in a state when you were late today.'

'Well when it happened a year ago Sam was confused and upset,' Lucy said, her voice husky as she spoke, 'and when I told him that Daddy wasn't coming back he was distraught. He couldn't understand how his Dad could have just left him there. He thought he must have done something naughty.'

Joel felt a red-hot anger burn through him. 'Does he see his father now?'

Lucy shook her head. 'I tried desperately hard to persuade Tim to stay in touch, for Sam's sake, but he wouldn't. He—' She broke off and coloured. 'He met someone else, you see. And I suppose they wanted a fresh start—I don't know…'

She reached into her pocket, pulled out a handkerchief and blew her nose sharply.

'Sorry.' She sniffed. 'Generally we're doing all right. It was just this afternoon I panicked.'

'I'm not surprised.'

Her love for her child touched something deep inside him.

'But it was all right.' She gave him a smile that he knew must have taken a lot of effort. 'I think he must be adjusting. He was upset at the time, as you saw, but he seemed all right this evening.'

'And what about you?' Joel couldn't help asking the question. 'Are you getting over it?'

'Well, leaving London and coming to Cornwall has been good,' she told him. 'My parents wanted me to move home and live with them, but I knew I couldn't do that. Sam and I are a family now and we have to learn to survive together.' She gave herself a little shake and changed the subject deftly. 'So, Dr Whittaker, are you going to stand there looking at me all night, or are you going to cook me something to eat?'

Her courage brought a lump to his throat but he forced himself to keep the atmosphere light since that was obviously what she wanted.

'*Something?*' He pretended to look offended. 'You call this gourmet creation of mine *something*? I can assure you, *madame*, it is a masterpiece of culinary invention.'

She smiled at him. 'Well, forgive me. I've never met a domesticated man before.'

He winked at her and threw some pasta into a pan of boiling water.

'Nick and Michael can cook, too. My mother taught all three of us to look after ourselves.'

Her expression was wistful. 'She's a lovely lady, your mother.'

'She certainly is.' Determined to make her relax with him, he kept up the small talk while he finished preparing the supper and then served it onto two plates which he carried through to the dining table. 'OK. Tuck in.'

She sat opposite him, occasionally glancing out of the huge window at the views of the harbour. 'I love this apartment. I'm amazed your parents have trouble letting it.'

Trouble letting it?

Joel opened his mouth to tell her that this particular apartment was always in demand, and then he realised just in time that his parents must have told her that because they'd known that otherwise she wouldn't have taken it.

And then she would have had nowhere to live.

Suddenly he was immensely proud of his parents. They were great people.

'Not many people want to come to Cornwall in the winter,' he hedged, shifting the conversation away from the subject of the flat. 'And what about you, Lucy? He topped up her wineglass and looked at her quizzically. 'Why did you choose Cornwall?'

'If you'd seen our flat in London, you wouldn't have to ask that,' she said with a rueful smile. 'Our money didn't go very far. And Sam's asthma got worse. I thought we needed a change and I saw this job advertised. I just didn't think for a moment that I'd get it.'

'Why not?'

'Because I'm a single parent,' she said simply. 'Working when you've got small children is hard at the best of times. Doing it when you're on your own with no support becomes a nightmare.'

'In what way?' He looked at her blankly. 'Surely once you've sorted out your child care, it's fine?' To be honest, he'd never given it a thought before.

Her eyes were bright with amusement. 'Spoken like a man with no children. I can assure you that it's far from fine. Working when you have a child just means that you are constantly torn between the two.'

'How come?' He leaned forward, his expression curious. 'Surely when you're at work you're working, and when Sam finishes school you're at home.'

It sounded straightforward enough to him.

'Unfortunately it's never quite as neat as that.' She gave a sigh and put her fork down. 'Patients don't observe the clock, and I'm horribly aware that I'm letting the practice down by not being able to give my all like everyone else. If there are extra patients I often have to refuse, and then I feel stressed and frustrated. If Sam is ill then the whole finely balanced show falls apart. I have to let people down at the last minute, and instead of just worrying about Sam being ill I'm also worrying about how I'm letting everyone down at work.'

Joel stared at her in silence, taking in everything she'd said. 'I'd never really thought about it before,' he admitted quietly. 'But I can see now that it must be a pretty stressful balancing act.'

'It's certainly that.' She gave a short laugh. 'Fortunately, your father is the kindest person I've ever met. If it weren't for him—' She broke off and Joel frowned, hating the fact that she was putting herself down.

'He hasn't taken you on out of charity, you know. You're a fantastic nurse, Lucy. And even in the short time

I've known you I can see that you get more done in the hours you work than many people do in double the time.'

Lucy gave a soft smile. 'Your father said the same thing earlier, but—'

'No buts. And don't fret about things that haven't happened, like Sam being off school. When it happens, we'll deal with it.'

Her eyes widened. 'We?'

He cleared his throat, as surprised as she was by what he'd said. What was he planning to do? Take care of the child himself?

He suddenly realised that he'd do exactly that if it would make things easier for her.

'You're part of a team, Lucy,' he said quietly, genuinely wanting to help. 'One of us would help and, yes, I'm quite prepared to be the one who takes care of Sam.'

She gave a soft laugh and shook her head slowly. 'What are you going to do? Take him on your calls with you?'

Joel gave it some thought. 'We could tuck him up in Reception with Ros. She looked after me on countless occasions when I was ill as a child.'

'She has a job to do,' Lucy pointed out, starting to laugh. 'Thank you for trying to help, but it really isn't your problem.'

He stared at her, thinking how gorgeous she looked when she smiled. 'What would you say if I wanted to make it my problem?'

'What are you, my knight in shining armour?' Her smile faded slowly. 'I didn't realise that riding a white charger was part of your job description, Dr Whittaker.'

'You know, you could drop the ''Dr Whittaker'' and call me Joel,' he suggested mildly, leaning back in his chair and finishing his wine. 'All this ''Doctor'' business is probably a little formal in the circumstances.'

'I prefer to call you Dr Whittaker.'

Joel was intrigued, and something about the tension in her narrow shoulders made his heart beat faster.

'What do you call Michael?'

'I call him Michael—but that's different…' A soft pink colour touched her cheekbones and suddenly his jeans felt uncomfortably tight.

She was so deliciously shy with him. It was hard to believe she'd been married and had a child.

'Why is it different, Lucy?'

There was a long silence and he could see her chest rising and falling as she breathed.

'Because Michael doesn't look at me the way you look at me.'

Her honest statement knocked the breath from his body, and although he knew he ought to drop the subject, he couldn't.

'And how do I look at you?'

Her colour deepened further and she didn't answer. Instead, she stood up quickly, picked up her plate and glass and escaped into the kitchen.

He was right behind her, standing in the doorway, digging his fingers into his palms to stop himself grabbing her.

'How do I look at you, Lucy?'

'Joel, please…' Her voice was choked and he kept his voice gentle.

'You call me Dr Whittaker because you're trying to keep me at a distance. The reason it feels different with Michael and Nick is because the chemistry isn't there. But there's something between us, Lucy, and there has been from the first moment we met.' He broke off and saw her take a deep breath.

'No.' She had her back to him and he took a step closer.

'Lucy—look at me. Look at me and tell me that you haven't felt it too.'

She didn't move. 'Maybe I have,' she said finally, her voice so low he could barely hear her, 'but it doesn't mean anything, Dr Whittaker.'

At least she wasn't denying it existed.

'Joel,' he corrected her softly, his voice amazingly steady considering how churned up he was inside, 'and it could mean something, Lucy.'

There was a long silence and he was aware of her soft breathing. 'I—I don't know what you want from me, but there isn't room in my life for any sort of relationship at the moment.'

Joel stared at the back of her head, unconsciously admiring the shiny black hair. He'd never met anyone quite like her before. He was used to women who flirted and played games, and Lucy did none of those things.

Realising that she was waiting for him to say something, he gently turned her to face him.

'How about friendship? Surely there's room in your life for that?'

She stared up at him and he noticed how beautiful her eyes were. An unusual shade of green surrounded by thick, dark lashes...

'Friendship? You don't strike me as the sort of man who usually settles for friendship.'

And she was right.

He looked her straight in the eye. 'I'm a fast learner.'

She shook her head and pulled away from him, her expression sceptical. 'I don't think so.'

'Are you telling me you don't need a friend?' He tried to keep his tone light. 'You're new to the area, Lucy. Dad tells me you never see anyone apart from at work and at school. Surely a bit of adult company would be welcome occasionally? If you feel low, you can cry on my shoulder. And if I feel low, I can do the same to you.'

She looked at him in silence, her eyes solemn. 'Answer me honestly. How many women friends have you had before? I mean friends that haven't been lovers.'

He licked his lips. 'Er—none,' he said finally, knowing that he couldn't lie to her. In fact, he'd never believed it was possible for a man and a woman to be just friends. At least, not until they'd got the sex out of the way.

She gave a gentle smile. 'I thought as much. No offence, but I don't really think you're friend material, Joel.'

'No?' He took a deep breath, racking his brains for a way to convince her. 'Who stole his brother's car to give you a lift to the school today when you were desperate? Who waited so that he could give you a lift home? Who checked your child when he had an asthma attack? Who just cooked you—?'

'Stop.' She lifted a hand and stopped him in mid-flow, her green eyes guilty. 'You're right, of course. I couldn't have had a better friend than you've been to me today. I don't know what I would have done without you.'

'Precisely.' He pretended to look offended. 'I may be new to this friendship lark, but I know the rules. And don't think I cook my special pasta dish for just anyone.'

She laughed at that, aware that he was teasing her. 'I'm honoured.'

'So what do you say?' He was deliberately keeping the conversation as light as possible so that he didn't scare her off. 'Will you give me the job? Chief friend? On a trial basis, of course. One foot wrong and you can fire me.'

She smiled and shook her head. 'You're crazy, do you know that?'

'Is that a yes?' He held his breath. At least she was still laughing.

'Just friends?'

'Just friends,' he said firmly, thinking that he might just be about to face the hardest challenge of his life.

'All right,' she said finally. 'Just as long as you promise not to cancel any hot dates on my behalf. It's purely friendship, Joel.'

He held up his hands. 'Absolutely. Friendship it is.'

She was still looking at him doubtfully. 'Are you sure you'll manage it?'

'Of course.'

He'd manage it if it killed him.

CHAPTER FIVE

'DAMMIT, Joel! We told you to leave her alone!' Michael smashed his fist onto Joel's desk and glared at him menacingly.

'Leave who alone?' Joel leaned back in his chair, his expression cool as he surveyed his brother.

'Don't play the innocent with me,' Michael growled. 'You know exactly what I'm talking about. You took my car—'

'You *gave* me your car,' Joel reminded him, and Michael frowned impatiently.

'All right, I gave you my car.' He waved a hand dismissively to show that it was a minor detail. 'But I didn't know you were going to try and make a move on Lucy.'

Joel's eyes were suddenly hard. 'I did not make a move on Lucy.'

'You took her home!'

Joel leaned back in his chair, his voice suddenly soft. 'Are you spying on me?'

'No! Well, yes—I suppose I am.' His normally calm older brother was unusually flustered. 'I wanted to know why you needed my car!' Michael lifted his hands in a gesture of pure exasperation. 'I saw you drive off with her.'

Joel looked at him steadily. 'Then you'll know that I gave Lucy a lift to the school to pick up Sam, because her own car wouldn't start.'

There was a long silence and Michael stared at him. 'You picked up Sam?'

'She was going to call a taxi,' Joel explained, wondering when his brother was going to leave him alone so that they could both get on with some work, 'and that would have made her very late. Not that any of this is your business.'

Why the hell was he explaining himself to his brother? He gave a wry smile. Maybe he was reminding himself of the facts. That he'd been helping Lucy—nothing more.

Michael was looking at him doubtfully. 'So you dropped her off home and then went upstairs to your own flat?'

'I didn't know you were so concerned for my virtue,' Joel drawled, controlling the irritation that threatened to bubble up inside him. 'I'm thirty-three years of age. I don't need my big brother to look out for me.'

'I'm not looking out for you,' Michael snarled. 'I'm looking out for Lucy!'

Joel's jaw tightened. And he knew why. It was because of the child, of course. Still, it galled him that his family had so little faith in his morals and ethics.

He leaned back in his chair and stared coldly at his brother. Suddenly he was fed up with being lectured. 'And why am I such a danger to Lucy?'

Michael gave him an impatient look. 'You know why! Lucy does not need to be messed around!'

Joel lifted an eyebrow speculatively. 'My, my, we are protective all of a sudden.'

Michael looked ready to explode and then caught the gleam in Joel's eye and subsided.

'Oh, damn you!' His smile was slightly sheepish. 'Well, maybe I am overreacting just a bit.'

'Just a bit.'

Michael coloured at the sarcasm in Joel's tone. 'Well, all right, then. More than just a bit. It's just that she— she—'

'She gets to you,' Joel finished softly, his eyes on his

brother as he leaned forward. 'There's something about the girl that makes you want to slay dragons and then take her back to your cave and keep her safe for ever.'

Michael pulled a face. 'Well, not exactly. Maria is already at home in my cave, and I don't want a black eye, but if you were speaking hypothetically, then, yes, I'd say you're spot on. Lucy Bishop seems to bring out everyone's protective instincts.' He hesitated and then gave a sigh. 'Look, I'm sorry for what I said. It's just that—'

'You don't trust me?' Joel's tone was soft and Michael gave a sigh.

'I've never interfered in your love life before—'

'Possibly because it is none of your business,' Joel pointed out pleasantly, and Michael looked at him, his eyes suddenly tired.

'Joel, with all your experience of women, surely you can see that Lucy is different. She's not one of your—' He broke off and Joel prompted him, his eyes suddenly narrowed.

'Yes?' His tone was smooth. 'She's not one of my…?'

'You know what I'm saying.' Michael waved a hand and gave his brother an exasperated look. 'Just don't go there, Joel! Don't mess the girl around.'

'Because I know that you mean well and have Lucy's interests at heart, I won't punch your lights out,' Joel said softly. 'And for the record, so that you don't lose sleep over it, I should tell you that I drove her home, I examined Sam, who had a mild asthma attack, and then I cooked her supper.'

There was a long silence while his brother digested that information.

'You cooked her supper?' Michael looked at him suspiciously. 'But Lucy's always refused to eat supper with any of us.'

'Well, she didn't refuse me.'

He didn't add that he hadn't given her much choice.

'And then what happened?'

Nothing, unfortunately.

Joel sighed. 'I went upstairs to my flat and slept in my own bed. Not that it's any of your damn business.'

'I thought we told you to leave her alone.'

There was a long silence and when Joel finally spoke his voice was very controlled. 'Firstly, you are not my keeper, and secondly, the girl needs a friend.'

Michael looked taken aback. 'A friend?'

Something inside Joel snapped. 'In case you hadn't noticed, she's struggling to manage a job and a child with less help than you get with your laundry! On top of that, it doesn't take a genius to see that she's lonely as hell. Yes, I'd say she needs a friend.'

'And you think that could be you?'

'And why not?'

'Since when have you ever had a female friend?'

Since last night.

'There's a first time for everything.'

'Oh, come off it, Joel!' Michael made an impatient sound. 'You don't know anything about being friends with a woman.'

'Well, I'm learning,' Joel said calmly. 'And the subject is now closed.'

Michael looked at him. 'Don't get mad with me. You're my brother and I love you, but Lucy is very vulnerable and you're very attractive to women—'

'You're afraid *she* might seduce *me*?'

'I'm afraid she might fall for you, yes,' Michael said quietly, ignoring Joel's mocking tone. 'And if that happened, I don't trust you to turn her away.'

Joel's mouth tightened. He wasn't sure he trusted himself either.

He took a deep breath. 'Relax,' he said wearily, wondering why the hell he was having this conversation with his brother. 'I have no intention of taking advantage of her, if that's what's worrying you. I'm really serious about just being her friend. I like her and I like the boy. Now, can we change the subject? I'm bored with this one.'

Michael gave a brief smile. 'I suppose so. I'm sorry if I was out of line, but—'

'But you couldn't help yourself,' Joel finished, giving a shake of his head as Michael strolled towards the door. 'How's little Millie, by the way?'

'Picking up.' Michael turned to look at him. 'According to the registrar, she's making good progress.'

'Did you speak to her today?'

'Last night.' Michael paused with his hand on the door. 'I visited them at the hospital and had a word with her while I was there.'

'You visited? Well, well.' A smile spread across Joel's face. 'My big brother is becoming an enormous softy.'

Michael didn't smile. 'That, and paranoid. I saw the child and missed the diagnosis, remember?'

'Rubbish.' Joel frowned sharply. He knew that his older brother was a perfectionist, but it hadn't occurred to him that he'd be blaming himself for not diagnosing Millie's illness sooner. 'You didn't miss anything. Every other doctor on the planet would have made the diagnosis you did.'

'What?' Michael laughed bitterly. 'Virus? Sometimes I wonder why I trained for all those years when all I do is say that word.'

'Don't beat yourself up,' Joel said calmly. 'You told her to come back if the temperature wasn't down; you told her to call if she was worried.'

'But she didn't,' Michael growled, and Joel nodded.

'And I guess that's what's hard about general practice. It's not like hospital, where you've got them captive and can run every test under the sun. You just have to make a judgement based on what you see. You saw a little girl with a temperature.'

'What makes you so wise all of a sudden?' Michael gave an awkward smile. 'You've only been in general practice for five minutes.'

'But I'm a man of the world, as you keep pointing out.' Joel locked eyes with his brother. 'You didn't do anything wrong. You told her to come back.'

Michael's gaze was troubled. 'But she didn't—'

'Yes, she did,' Joel pointed out. 'She came to see Lucy—who is, by the way, one hell of a great practice nurse.'

Michael nodded agreement. 'Yes, well, we certainly agree on that. She's a bright girl. And she did well, spotting Millie's problem.'

'It's called teamwork, bro.' Joel stood up and walked over to Michael, giving him a friendly punch on the shoulder. 'You're a great doctor. Don't forget it. And you're still my hero even if you are an interfering pain in the neck.'

'That sounded more like an insult than a compliment,' Michael drawled, a smile touching his mouth, and Joel put a hand on his chest and faked an injured expression.

'Me? Insult my brother? Never.'

'Of course, never.' Michael gave a wry smile before stepping into the corridor and closing the door behind him.

Joel watched him go, his smile fading rapidly as he thought back over their conversation. He hadn't admitted it to Michael, but it had taken all his will power to leave

Lucy last night. What he'd really wanted to do was drag her down onto the floor and have his wicked way with her.

The chemistry between them was so powerful it took his breath away, and all Joel's experience with women told him that she felt it, too. But he knew that it wouldn't make any difference. She'd been terribly hurt, and although he'd never claimed to be an expert in the way women's minds worked, you didn't need a degree in female psychology to know that she wasn't going to be interested in men.

Especially a man like him who didn't seem to be able to settle down with one woman.

Which meant that he was going to have to learn to keep his feelings under control.

He gave a groan and ran a hand over his face. Judging from the way his body reacted even when he thought about her, it was going to be easier said than done.

Lucy checked her watch again and hoped for the hundredth time that morning that Sam was OK.

He'd certainly seemed all right when she'd dropped him at school. She'd checked his peak flow and had decided that he was well enough to go. But it didn't stop her worrying. At least the class teacher had promised to call if she was worried.

She worked her way steadily through her hypertension clinic, checking blood pressures, giving dietary advice, and it was lunchtime when Joel walked into the room.

He stood aside to let her last patient out of the room and then closed the door so that they were alone.

'How's Sam?'

Lucy tossed an old bandage in the bin and gave him a shy smile. 'He seems OK. I'm glad you popped in. I wanted to thank you again for last night.'

'No thanks needed. How was he after I left? Did he wake up? Any bad dreams?'

She was touched by his concern. 'Actually, he slept well. I was expecting problems but he was fine once we talked about it.' She felt nothing but relief that after the initial shock Sam had seemed all right. 'I suppose he's grown up a lot in the last year. Children understand things at six that they don't understand when they're five.'

Joel gave a rueful smile. 'I can't honestly claim any great experience with children that age, but I'm sure you're right. Look—we still haven't talked about the asthma and immunisation clinics. I'm keen to hear what you think.'

Lucy glanced at her appointments on the computer. 'My next patient has cancelled. We could have a quick chat now, if that suits you.'

He nodded, and Lucy quickly ran through the routine for the asthma clinic, stumbling over her words as she tried hard to concentrate and not notice how handsome he was.

She didn't understand her reaction to him. It wasn't as if she was looking for a relationship. Far from it.

After Tim had left she'd never thought for a moment that one day she might be interested in a man again, but here she was thinking all sorts of shocking thoughts just because she'd met someone who was extremely good-looking.

But she was glad that she'd insisted they just be friends. She wasn't ready to cope with anything more.

Joel was considering what she'd told him about the asthma clinic. 'So you're trained to do spirometry?'

Lucy nodded. 'As you know, we have lots of elderly patients in the practice and there's an increase in respiratory diseases. It's important that we distinguish between asthma and chronic obstructive airways disease because the treatment is different, and spirometry is important for that.'

'And the immunisation clinic?'

Lucy ran him through the format for the clinic and he listened carefully.

'The mothers get sent the appointment automatically?'

'Yes.'

'And if they don't turn up?'

'They get sent another one,' Lucy said promptly. 'And Kim, the health visitor, sometimes follows them up.'

Joel lifted an eyebrow. 'Sometimes?'

'Well, chasing non-attenders isn't really her role,' Lucy said. 'Of course, she talks to them all about immunisation at the birth visit, and whenever she sees them, but she doesn't spend her day chasing after people who don't turn up.'

'Right.' Joel looked at her thoughtfully. 'So have you had any ideas?'

Lucy blushed. 'Well, yes…'

'Go on,' he prompted, his expression suddenly interested. 'I want to know what you think.'

Lucy took a deep breath. 'What I think,' she said slowly, 'is that instead of running an immunisation clinic, we should run a child health clinic.'

'Isn't that what we do?'

Lucy shook her head. 'No, it isn't. We invite mothers to come and have their babies jabbed and that's it.'

Joel sat down on one of her chairs and looked at her expectantly. 'So what are you proposing?'

Lucy warmed to her theme. 'Well, it seems to me that because all we offer is immunisation, if people have any doubts they don't come. If we widen the scope of the clinic we might attract a different set of people. A child health clinic would be exactly that—a chance to come and talk about your child's health. A chance to ask all those little questions that worry you but that aren't enough to make you see a doctor.'

'But surely those people just ring the health visitor?'

'No.' Lucy shook her head again. 'Usually they just struggle on or ask each other. And that's the other thing— we could use the clinic as a support network for the mothers. There's not much going on here in the winter and lots of the new mothers feel isolated. If we run it over the lunchtime and early afternoon, when there are no surgeries, they can chat together and use the waiting room as a meeting place. We can arrange for a speaker once a month and get some extra toys—' She broke off and he smiled.

'I can see you've really been thinking about this.'

She gave him a hesitant smile. 'I just think that if we can be a place where mothers meet and drop in with any health worries, we can talk to them about immunisation at the same time. A GP always has to be on the premises when we give the immunisations, so we might as well use you! They can come and see the doctor on a first come, first served basis instead of having to make an appointment.'

Joel was silent for a moment, thinking it through. 'It's a good idea. In fact, it's better than that. It's a brilliant idea. Have you run it past Dad?'

Lucy shook her head. 'No. I didn't really think we could make it work, but now with an extra partner...'

'Would the health visitors agree, do you think?'

Lucy nodded. 'I did mention it in passing to Kim and she was all for it. Anything that gets the immunisation rates up.'

'All right.' Joel stood up and raked long fingers through his cropped hair. 'I'll have a word with Dad, but it sounds a great idea to me.'

'Let me know what he says.' Lucy tucked her hair behind her ears and then gasped. 'Oh—I almost forgot. What do I owe you for sorting out my car?'

He'd dropped the keys round that morning, assuring her that the car was now fine, but he'd dashed off so quickly she'd barely had time to thank him.

'Nothing. It was a simple problem and it shouldn't happen again.'

'Well, thank you.' She gave a hesitant smile. 'And thank you for dinner. It was a real treat to be cooked for. Sam and I owe you a meal.'

He shook his head. 'You don't owe me anything,' he said slowly. 'Friends cook each other meals all the time. It's no big deal.'

'I'd really like to. Sam's favourite gourmet treat is sausages.' She was laughing now. 'I assume that would meet with your approval?'

'I adore sausages.' He patted his flat stomach. 'With mash and onion gravy. Now, I'd better get back to work. I'll see you later.'

Lucy watched him go, feeling lighter inside than she had for a long time. As well as being dangerously good-looking, Joel Whittaker was a thoroughly nice man.

But he was just a friend, she reminded herself. And that was all a man like Joel would ever be.

This was never going to work.

Joel sank into his chair and closed his eyes.

He might have assured Lucy that he could learn to be a friend, but he was fairly sure that friends weren't supposed to have the sort of thoughts that he'd been having.

The truth was that he wasn't sure he could trust himself to have dinner with her again, even if Sam was there. He was afraid that if he was alone in a room with her he'd give in to his baser instincts and kiss her senseless.

He was sitting brooding at his desk when the door opened.

'Are you all right?' Richard Whittaker frowned at him. 'Something worrying you?'

Yes—but nothing he could share with his father.

'I'm fine. I'm glad you've popped in,' he said briskly. 'Lucy's come up with a good idea for the immunisation clinic—I wanted to run it past you.'

Briefly he outlined Lucy's proposal, and his father listened carefully.

'Sounds a good idea to me.' Richard settled himself in a vacant chair and nodded his approval. 'I can't think why it wouldn't work, but I suppose we ought to discuss it with everyone. We really need to discuss it at the next practice meeting.'

'We can't do that.' Joel shook his head emphatically. 'It's at five o'clock on Friday and Lucy has to leave at three to pick Sam up from school. It wouldn't be fair to ask her.'

In the short time that he'd known her she'd made it clear that Sam came first. And quite right, too...

Richard frowned. 'I'd forgotten about her leaving at three.' He pondered the problem for a moment and Joel glanced briefly at his diary.

'What about Saturday lunchtime?'

'The weekend? I don't think so.' His father looked doubtful. 'We've invited her over before and she's always refused.'

'Get Nick and Michael there, tell her it's a practice meeting and she'll come,' Joel said confidently, flipping his diary shut with a careless finger. 'Provided she can bring Sam, of course.'

His father's eyes narrowed. 'You think she'll say yes?'

Joel looked him straight in the eye. 'Lucy is far too conscientious to refuse to attend a work meeting.'

He listened while his father spoke to Lucy on the phone and stiffened slightly as he heard her soft tap on the door moments later.

'Ah, there you are, my dear.' Richard stepped forward and put an arm around her shoulders, drawing her into the room. 'Joel's been outlining your suggestions for the immunisation clinic. We need to work through the detail with everyone. We have a practice meeting on Friday evening, but I know you can't make that.'

Lucy bit her lip and looked troubled, just as Joel had known she would. She was incredibly conscientious.

'I'm sorry—'

'Don't be sorry,' Richard said immediately. 'We were hoping you might be able to do Saturday lunchtime instead. Bring Sam—we'll find plenty for him to do at the house.'

Even though she was a small distance away from him, Joel could just detect the soft scent that he'd come to associate with her. What was it? He wouldn't be surprised if it was something as simple as shampoo.

Lucy was staring at his father. 'Saturday?'

'If that's convenient for you,' Richard said cheerfully. 'Elizabeth will cook one of her lunches and we can all chat while we eat. It happens all the time in our house. Being a family practice inevitably means that we're always mixing business and pleasure.'

'Do I really need to be there?' Her green eyes reflected her uncertainty and Joel wondered why she hated going out so much.

'It's your idea that we're discussing and developing,'

Richard pointed out. 'If you're worried about Sam, don't be. There'll be plenty of people to entertain him.'

'All right, then,' she said finally, finding a smile that did nothing to hide her uncertainty. She slid her fingers nervously through her sleek hair. 'I—I don't know where the house is. You'll have to give me a map.'

'I'll drive you,' Joel said immediately, reflecting with wry humour that he seemed to have a need to torture himself.

His father frowned slightly and Joel met his gaze without flinching, knowing that he could expect another lecture later.

And maybe they were right to lecture him.

They were certainly right that he was unsuitable for Lucy. She certainly wasn't the sort of woman who enjoyed casual flings, and the last thing on his mind was commitment.

Which just left friendship.

And that was proving harder than he'd imagined.

'Lucy, that's inspired!' Richard sat back in his chair at the lunch table and stared at her admiringly. 'Why did none of us think of that?'

'What sort of talks did you have in mind, Lucy?' Michael helped himself to another roast potato and glanced across at her. 'Child-centred things—weaning, teething…?'

'Well, we could do that,' Lucy said hesitantly, and Joel looked at her searchingly.

'But you've got a better idea?'

'The problem is that those sorts of talks attract mothers who are already very motivated and interested. I think we should cover those issues, of course, but also broaden it out. Cover topics that are more frivolous, more of general interest.' Lucy realised that they were all watching her, and blushed slightly. 'Maybe we should cover topics that are more personal.'

'Such as?'

'Well, one of Fiona's mothers is a fitness instructor—she could talk to them about getting into shape with small children.' Lucy bit her lip, wondering whether it was a stupid idea. 'I mean, I know it's hard when you've got toddlers, but there are exercises that you can do around the home. I also thought we could maybe have some talks on clothes or make-up—something that's for them.'

Elizabeth beamed at her. 'That's a brilliant idea. They'll come along for a gossip and to learn something, and while they're there we'll talk to them about immunisation.'

'That's right.'

'I can't think why none of us have thought of it before.' Elizabeth held up her wineglass. 'A toast to Lucy. An asset to our practice.'

'Lucy…' they chorused, and she smiled self-consciously.

'Well, if you're sure you approve, I'll get together and plan it with Fiona.'

'Ros can help you design some posters,' Nick said. 'She's a genius with the computer.'

Michael put down his knife and fork and sat back in his chair. 'So what day are we going to do it?'

'Thursdays,' Joel said immediately. 'It has to fit around the other clinics and that seems as good a time as any.'

They talked through the details and Lucy found herself relaxing and joining in, enjoying the flow of conversation and ideas. The Whittakers were all very bright; there was no doubt about that.

'Mum.' Sam's little voice interrupted them in mid-flow. 'When are we going home?'

Lucy blushed with mortification but Joel laughed.

'Sorry, old chap. We must have been boring you to tears, but you've been so good and quiet there we all forgot about you.'

'The poor child!' Elizabeth gave a gasp of apology and jumped to her feet. 'You come into the kitchen with me, Sam, and we'll see what we can find in my cupboards. I kept lots of toys from when my boys were small.'

Lucy sneaked a glance at the three powerfully built men who were lounging around the table. She couldn't imagine any of them as children.

Joel caught her eye and grinned. 'I was a cute baby. Want to see the photos of me in the bath?'

She knew he was teasing her but still blushed, and Nick came to her rescue.

'Why on earth would the girl want to see photos of you in the bath? Disgusting, if you ask me.'

Joel looked affronted. 'I was a beautiful baby.'

Nick looked at him through narrowed eyes. 'They always say that the past is no predictor of the future, and in this case they were obviously right.'

Richard coughed pointedly. 'So what's happening this afternoon? We've already bored little Sam rigid. We ought to do something to entertain him.'

'Oh, there's no need,' Lucy said quickly, folding her serviette carefully and placing it back on the table. 'Lunch was delicious, and it was good to chat, but we'll be off home in a minute.'

Nick shook his head. 'You haven't sampled Mum's puddings yet.'

Sam came back with Elizabeth, clutching a huge basket full of toys. 'Wow, Mum. Look at this train. It's so cool.'

Lucy caught Joel grinning and smiled, too. It was nice to see Sam so happy.

'That was Nick's.' Elizabeth knelt on the floor next to the child and sorted through the toys with him. 'Oh, I didn't know we still had this—look at this, Richard. Your father bought this for Michael on his fifth birthday.'

Happily involved with the toys, Sam showed no inclination to leave. And once Elizabeth had served dessert, the conversation moved on to the Valentine's Ball that Elizabeth was planning.

'We've sold a hundred tickets,' she told them proudly. 'It's going to be the best night ever and we're going to make a fortune!'

Lucy smiled. 'Who is it in aid of?'

'The lifeboat,' Elizabeth said immediately, reaching for the cream and pouring some on her pudding. 'We make a profit on the tickets and then hold an auction and several other things during the evening to make money. Will you come?'

Lucy shook her head immediately, searching for a ready excuse. 'I've got no one to look after Sam.'

She'd never been to a ball in her life. Neither did she want to. Especially not a Valentine's Ball. It would be full of romantic couples, reminding her what a hopeless mess her life was in.

'Maria could look after Sam,' Michael suggested, helping himself to more pudding. 'I'm on call, so we're not going.'

Maria smiled. 'I'd be very happy to.'

Lucy searched for another excuse to avoid telling them the truth. 'I haven't got anything to wear.'

Tina smiled. 'I own a boutique, remember? And I happen to have just the thing—it would look stunning with your dark hair.'

Lucy started to feel panicky. She didn't want to go to a ball. It would be full of loving couples and she couldn't bear being near loving couples. It just reminded her too painfully of what she and Sam had lost.

To her relief and surprise, Joel intervened.

'Leave the girl alone,' he said smoothly. 'If Lucy wants to go to the ball, she can ask for a ticket. She doesn't need a fairy godmother. Talking of lifeboats, I gather they had a dramatic rescue last weekend. Three teenagers were swept off the rocks.'

Knowing that he'd changed the subject on her behalf, Lucy shot Joel a grateful look and listened with interest as the conversation turned to the lifeboat rescue.

'Yeah.' Nick nodded slowly. 'They scrambled a rescue helicopter and sent out the all-weather lifeboat. Those rocks are lethal, and unfortunately people don't realise how quickly the tide comes in.'

They spent the rest of the afternoon happily chatting and eating while Sam amused himself with the toys Elizabeth had found for him.

Eventually, though, it was time to leave, and when they drove back to the harbour Sam was fast asleep in the back seat of Joel's car.

He scooped the sleeping child into his arms and carried him out of the car and up into Lucy's flat.

'His bedroom's through there...' Lucy gestured down the hallway and Sam shouldered the door open and laid the child on the bed.

'I'll undress him in a minute.' She covered Sam with a fleecy throw to keep him warm and turned to find Joel leaning against the doorframe, his blue eyes watching her every move. 'He had such a great time. Thank you.'

In the confines of Sam's bedroom, his shoulders seemed broader than ever and his powerful frame seemed to fill the doorway.

'You're welcome.'

The darkness created an intimacy that made her heart rate increase.

Just friends, she reminded herself.

'Come and have a coffee.'

She pushed past him, ignoring the feel of his hard thighs as she brushed against him.

Walking through to the kitchen, she flicked on the kettle and smiled at him. 'I wanted to thank you for rescuing me earlier. Your family were determined that I was going to go to the ball.'

'And you didn't want to.'

'No.' She shook her head slowly. 'Not my sort of thing.'

There was a slight pause. 'Not even with a friend?'

Her eyes flew to his and her heart beat faster. 'Are you asking me to go to the ball with you?'

'I haven't anyone to go with.'

His pathetic expression didn't fool her and she laughed and gave him a wry look. 'You really expect me to believe that, Dr Whittaker?'

'Are you saying you don't?' He folded his arms and gave her a sexy smile. 'All right, then, let's just say that one has to be very careful who one takes to the Valentine's Ball. They might get the wrong idea.'

In other words, he didn't want some poor woman thinking he was serious about her.

She shook her head reprovingly. 'So I'm supposed to be going to protect you?'

'Definitely.' He nodded vigorously. 'Think of yourself as a bodyguard. You're going to be guarding my body.'

She smiled hesitantly, horrified to find herself wondering what his body was like under his stylish clothes. Firm, well muscled, totally male...

She swallowed and poured hot water onto the coffee. 'I don't think a ball is really my scene...'

'You need to go out, Lucy,' he said quietly. 'When did you last have some fun?'

She stood still. She couldn't remember.

'They have a fantastic live band. We can dance till our feet are blistered.'

She laughed. 'And that's supposed to be a good thing?'

'Don't you like dancing?'

'Joel, I'm a mother with a child of six.'

'So?' He shrugged, clearly at a loss to see the relevance of her statement. 'Since when did having a child stop you dancing? Say yes, Lucy. I guarantee you'll have a good time.'

Dancing…

Suddenly her heart felt lighter than it had for a long time.

An evening dancing with Joel sounded fun.

'All right.' She looked at him, still unable to believe that she'd just said yes. 'But don't blame me if I tread on your toes.'

He grinned and picked up his coffee. 'I'll wear metal toecaps.'

She watched him walk out of the kitchen and wondered what she'd just said yes to.

An evening of fun, that was all, she told herself firmly.

Joel was right. It was too long since she'd had fun.

CHAPTER SIX

Two weeks later Joel had come to the conclusion that being Lucy's friend was the hardest thing he'd ever done in his life.

He'd lost count of the number of times he'd nearly kissed her.

Foolishly, he'd taken to ambling down to her apartment once Sam was in bed and they'd share a bottle of wine and talk until late in the evening. Sometimes she invited him down at teatime and he played with Sam, gradually getting to know the boy.

Lucy was slowly relaxing and opening up to him, but that just seemed to make things worse.

The more he knew her, the more he wanted her.

But he knew she was enjoying their friendship—needed their friendship—and he had no intention of letting her down.

Which meant that he had to keep his male urges well under control.

With a groan he switched on his computer and stared at the screen, acknowledging that he was in big trouble.

He had a mountain of work to do and all he could think about was Lucy.

He'd been out with a fair number of women in his time but he couldn't honestly remember a single one that had interfered with his concentration like Lucy did.

What was it about her?

She wasn't the first woman in the world to have a pretty

face and a gentle personality. But she was the first woman to have affected him this strongly.

And now he needed to talk to her about a patient, which meant another agonising session of trying not to kiss her.

With a sigh he rose from his desk and left his room.

He rapped on her door and came straight to the point. 'You did mention that you were trained to do spirometry, didn't you?'

Lucy nodded, clearly startled by his direct approach. He could hardly blame her for that. It was customary to say good morning or something similar when you first met a colleague, but he was desperately trying to keep his mind on work and not to look at her soft mouth.

'W-why are you asking about spirometry?'

Spirometry was a method of assessing lung function and was an important tool for monitoring the progress of patients with asthma or COPD.

'I've got a patient who needs it.'

Lucy nodded. 'We have quite a few patients who were diagnosed with asthma and then developed chronic obstructive pulmonary disease—as you know, it's hard to distinguish one from the other. Who do you want me to see?'

Joel perched himself on the edge of her desk and forced himself to concentrate on work. 'Margaret Patterson. She's sixty-one. She came to see me this morning with a chest infection, but when I had a chat with her she admitted that she has trouble walking as fast as she used to because she gets so breathless, and she can't hold a conversation and walk at the same time.'

Lucy tilted her head to one side as she listened. 'Is she a smoker?'

Joel grimaced. 'Fifteen to twenty a day. I listened to her chest and she had some basal crepitations and a wheeze so I've given her some antibiotics and asked her to make an appointment with you for spirometry.'

'Would she stop smoking, do you think? We could ask Janice to see her.'

Janice, the other practice nurse, ran the stop-smoking clinic and she and Lucy worked closely together.

'Well, I've suggested it, but I'm not sure if she'll do it,' Joel said, a resigned expression on his handsome face. 'What we really need to find out is whether this is asthma or COPD. It can be pretty hard to distinguish between the two, as you know, but it's important because the management is different.'

'Yes, absolutely.' Lucy nodded. 'Has she made an appointment with me?'

'This afternoon.'

He stood up and gave her a brief nod before leaving the room, steeling himself not to look at the swell of her breasts or the curve of her hips.

Margaret attended for her spirometry testing that afternoon and Lucy started off by talking her through her history. She established that Margaret had no history of chest problems or wheezing illness in childhood, and that she'd been fit and active.

'And what sort of work did you do, Mrs Patterson?'

Lucy was aware that COPD was associated with some occupations, but as the patient ran through her career history it was obvious that there was nothing that could be held responsible for her current breathing problems.

'Call me Margaret, please. As for having trouble breathing, I only really notice it when I get colds,' Margaret told her. 'It doesn't keep me awake at night, although I do cough in the morning, but I've always assumed that was because of my disgusting habit. I don't really understand why I have to have this test. I've had my peak flow measured before. Isn't that enough?'

Lucy shook her head. 'What we're trying to do is work out whether you have asthma or something called COPD. That stands for chronic obstructive pulmonary disease. It's another form of obstructive airway disease and it's closely related to smoking. A single peak-flow reading won't really show us if the air flow through the small airways is reduced. What we need to do is measure what we call the forced expired volume in one second—in other words, the amount of air you can blow out after you've breathed in deeply.'

Margaret gave a resigned shrug. 'All right, then, let's get on with it. Where do I blow?'

Lucy smiled. 'Not so fast. First I need to check your weight, height and blood pressure. I enter some of the data into the spirometer to enable us to calculate the test results.'

Margaret obligingly rolled up her sleeve and Lucy took the necessary recordings.

'All right.' Lucy entered the data into the spirometer. 'Now I need you to hold it…like this… Great.'

Lucy explained how Margaret should use the spirometer, but as the patient blew into the machine she had an uncontrollable fit of coughing.

'Oh, I'm so sorry.' Margaret broke off as another fit of coughing took hold of her and Lucy fetched her a glass of water.

'Here—try this. Don't worry about it. People often can't do it when they've had a chest infection. What we probably need to do is leave it two weeks to give the antibiotics time to work. In the meantime, I'd like you to record your peak flow several times a day. That will help us decide on the best method of treatment.'

Margaret sank into the chair and ran a hand over her forehead. 'I never thought I'd hear myself say this, but I think I need to talk to someone about the smoking.' She slumped in the chair, looking worn out and defeated. 'To be honest, I thought I was too old to give up, but this cough has been awful. I don't want to have another infection like this one.'

Lucy was sympathetic. 'It is really hard giving up smoking, but people do succeed, Margaret, particularly if they're really motivated. Having a severe chest infection just might be the trigger for you.'

Mary looked resigned. 'So what's the most effective way of going about it?'

Lucy smiled, pleased that she was even considering it. 'You need to talk to my colleague, Janice. She runs a stop smoking-clinic and she's had some amazing successes. Basically, it's a mixture of counselling in groups, individual sessions and nicotine replacement. She's done a booklet on it for the practice. I'll get one for you on your way out.'

She talked to Margaret for a few more minutes and then walked with her back to the waiting room and found her the booklet. Then she went to find Joel.

She found him in his consulting room, on the internet.

He glanced up with a smile as she walked into the room. 'Where did we get our information before the internet?'

Relieved that he seemed more relaxed than he had earlier, Lucy walked round behind him so that she could see the screen, watching with fascination as he searched for the information he wanted.

'That's amazing. I confess I'm not that confident about using the internet,' she said, her eyes widening in surprise at the quality of the information he'd managed to access.

'That's fantastic. Can anyone go on that website? Is it free?'

He nodded. 'This particular one is free, but it's password protected so it isn't open to the public. I had to register. But there are plenty of good medical websites, and lots of the journals have their own websites with archives that you can search. I can't imagine wading through books and paper any more.'

Standing so close to him, Lucy was suddenly very aware of the width of his shoulders. He was wearing one of the dark poloneck jumpers that he favoured, and his subtle male scent teased her nostrils.

Suddenly anxious to put some distance between them, she backed away and moved back behind the relative safety of his desk.

'I wanted to talk to you about Margaret.'

'Oh, yes?' He sat back and looked at her expectantly. 'What happened?'

'She was coughing too badly to do the spirometry so she's going to make another appointment for two weeks' time.'

Joel nodded. 'I thought that might happen, but it was worth a try. In the meantime, I'm sending her for a chest X-ray. She is a smoker, so I want to exclude lung cancer and heart failure and I sent off some bloods. She doesn't look anaemic but it's worth checking because it could be the cause of her breathlessness.'

Lucy nodded. 'You'll be pleased to hear that she's going to try and stop smoking.'

Joel raised his eyebrows. 'Pleased and surprised. I must admit I didn't think there was any hope of that.'

'I think the chest infection scared her.'

'Did it now?' Joel looked at her thoughtfully. 'So we

need to strike while the iron is hot. Did she make an appointment to see Janice?'

Lucy shook her head. 'No, she wasn't that committed. She wanted to go away and read the leaflets first. I think even considering giving up smoking is a big step for her.'

'OK.' Joel nodded slowly. 'In that case, I'll give her a call in a few days to check on her and to give her a little push.'

Joel caught up with Lucy a few days later. 'I just wanted to tell you that I had the results of Margaret's chest X-ray.'

Lucy looked at him. 'And?'

'It showed some evidence of pulmonary hyperinflation.'

'Oh.' Lucy pulled a face, 'That's caused by air trapping, isn't it? It's a typical feature of COPD, but it can occur in chronic asthma so I suppose we still don't have a diagnosis. What about her other tests?'

'Her heart size was normal and there was no evidence of any other pathology.'

'I've asked her to do serial peak-flow readings so when she comes back we can look at those results,' Lucy suggested.

Joel nodded approval. 'Good idea.'

That afternoon Lucy worked with Kim, the health visitor, to develop the idea for the new child health clinic.

Ros had designed a poster which they all agreed was fantastic, and Kim spread the word among the mothers as she went about her calls.

'Never suggest anything in this practice,' Joel said cheerfully one morning when they met in the staffroom. 'From having to be present while you jab babies, I'm now the one that's lumbered with being the doctor for the child health clinic.'

Lucy looked at him guiltily. 'Do you mind, really?'

'Of course not. I think it's a great idea, and I suppose it's sensible to have some consistency. Have you arranged a speaker for the first meeting?'

'Actually, yes.' Lucy nodded. 'One of Kim's mothers is an image consultant and she's agreed to come and talk about colours and things.'

Joel's expression was comical. 'Remind me to hide in my surgery. It all sounds terrifying.'

'You're certainly not going to hide in your surgery,' said Kim briskly as she walked past and overheard the conversation. 'We agreed that you'd mingle, remember? Be there to answer little questions that worry people.'

Joel groaned. 'Why did I ever agree to this?'

But his smile was good-natured and Lucy knew that he was pleased to help.

'If you're good, we'll let you have five minutes with the image consultant,' Lucy teased, 'just in case you're wearing the wrong colours for your skin tone.'

In fact, the image consultant was a great success, and the turnout was greater than Lucy and Kim had hoped for in their wildest dreams.

'Can you believe the Porter family are here?' Kim muttered to Lucy in an undertone as they checked the list of children for vaccination. 'I've never managed to persuade her to come to clinic before. I can't believe that an image consultant and a free cup of coffee was all it took.'

'It's nothing to do with the image consultant or the coffee,' Ros said dryly. 'It's Joel. They've all come to see him.'

Lucy and Kim exchanged looks, startled, and then both turned to look at where Joel was standing, surrounded by a group of giggling mothers.

'I think you just might be right, Ros,' Kim said softly. 'Oh, well, whatever it takes.'

They spent the rest of the session giving immunizations to little ones and advice to mothers, and when the last mother finally left they looked at each other in disbelief.

'We had five babies who've never been immunised before,' Ros said slowly, looking at her list. 'That's amazing.'

Joel nodded. 'It was a great idea, Lucy.'

Lucy shook her head. 'It wasn't me, it was you. They came to see you.'

Joel frowned briefly and then shrugged. 'Just as long as they're gentle with me.'

He gave her a wink that was so sexy it made her insides lurch uncomfortably.

'House calls, Dr Heartthrob,' Ros teased, waving some notes in his direction. 'One of them is Millie Gordon. She's been discharged from hospital and Michael wanted to call on her, but he's been tied up with a man with chest pain for an hour. He wondered if you'd go.'

'Gladly.' Joel put out his hands for the notes and looked at Lucy. 'Want to come with me as she was your patient?'

Lucy looked at the clock and bit her lip. It was already two o'clock. She didn't have patients booked in for the afternoon and she'd planned to do some restocking, but still...

'They don't live far away. I'll have you at the school at three, and that's a promise,' Joel said softly, clearly reading her mind.

'All right, then.' She nodded and smiled. 'I'd really like that.'

She grabbed her coat and followed him to his car, a brand-new BMW.

'Is it better than the motorbike?' She slid into the passenger seat and cuddled her coat around her. The weather was still bitterly cold.

'Well, it's a lot warmer,' Joel said, his teeth gritted as he started the engine and shivered. 'Or at least it is once the engine warms up.'

Millie and her family lived in one of the tiny fishermen's cottages. Joel and Lucy walked down the path together towards the front door, and rang the bell. After a minute or so Millie's mother opened the door, and her face brightened. 'Oh—I wasn't expecting you to call. How nice.'

'Dr Michael wanted to come,' Joel told her, 'but he's dealing with an emergency so you're landed with me instead. He sent his best wishes and told you to call him, day or night, if you're worried. Talking of which, how are things?'

'Well, it feels a bit strange, Millie being home from hospital,' Mrs Gordon confessed. 'I feel a bit nervous that it's all my responsibility now, but she seems fine. I suppose they wouldn't have discharged her if she wasn't.'

'That's right,' Joel agreed, following her into the sitting room and grinning at Millie. 'Hello, trouble. How are you doing?'

'I've been in hothpital,' the little girl lisped, her cheeks dimpling as she smiled.

'I know you have.' Joel nodded and dropped to his haunches next to the little girl. 'What was it like?'

'Fun. I did you a painting.'

'You did a painting for me?' A strange expression crossed Joel's face and he cleared his throat. 'Well—that's great. Thank you. Can I see it?'

Millie nodded and wriggled off the sofa, padding across the room to the table at the far end.

'I did one for you, too.' She handed a brightly coloured blur to Lucy. 'Because you saved me.'

Lucy felt a lump build in her throat. 'Thank you, Millie,' she said softly, stooping to hug the little girl. 'This is beautiful. I shall put it on my kitchen wall at home. That way I'll see it every morning when I eat my breakfast.'

Millie looked pleased and she turned to Joel. 'Where will you put yours?'

'The kitchen sounds like a great idea,' he agreed. 'Above my table. Thank you, Millie. No one's ever painted me a picture before.'

Joel turned to Millie's mother. 'Did the hospital give you a letter for us?'

The woman nodded and nipped out of the room. She was back within a minute and handed Joel a brown envelope. He opened it and read the contents.

'So they've arranged a follow-up appointment at the paediatric clinic. That's good. All right, Millie, let's take a little look at you.'

He examined Millie and they chatted a little longer. Finally Joel glanced at his watch and stood up.

'We'll leave you in peace now, but remember—any problems, call the surgery.'

'Thanks very much, Dr Whittaker.'

Millie's mother walked with them to the door and waved them off.

'Nice woman,' Joel said as they climbed back into the car and drove towards the school. 'You can relax—we'll be in plenty of time.'

Lucy gave him a grateful smile. 'Thanks, Joel. If you drop us back at the surgery I can pick my car up and drive us home. Do you want to join us for supper tonight?'

Joel cleared his throat, his tone casual. 'I've got a better idea. Why don't I take us all out instead? Sticky milkshakes and hamburgers?'

Lucy looked at him with an expression of disbelief. 'You eat hamburgers?'

'Well, no', he confessed with a rueful smile, 'not usually, but I can learn. I want to take you and Sam out for tea.'

Lucy stared at him. 'Aren't you working?'

'No.' Joel shook his head. 'Time off for good behaviour. So what do you say—is it a date? I mean, not a real date, of course,' he said, correcting himself hastily, 'just a date as in tea with friends.'

'Relax, Joel. There's no chance I'd mistake this for a real date,' she joked. 'I shouldn't think that your idea of a date is a hamburger at four o'clock in the afternoon.'

He grinned. 'Well, maybe not.'

They stopped at Lucy's flat just long enough for her to change out of her uniform into a pair of comfortable jeans and a blue jumper, and then drove to the school.

Sam was the first child out of the door and he dashed across the playground and stood on tiptoe to hug his mother.

'Guess what?' He was so excited he could hardly talk. 'There's a theatre company coming to school tomorrow and some of the children can take part. I might be one of them.'

'That's great, sweetheart.' She hugged him close, a feeling of warmth spreading through her veins as she felt his excitement. It had been a good idea to move to Cornwall. He was settling in so well.

'Hi, Joel.' Sam looked at Joel and gave a shy grin. 'Are you having supper with us again tonight?'

Joel shook his head and stuffed his hands deep into his coat pockets to keep them warm. 'No. I'm taking us all out instead. On a trip.'

'A trip?' Sam's face brightened at the thought. 'We normally go straight home after school.'

'Not today. Today we're going on a mystery tour.'

Sam's eyes widened and he smiled with delight. 'Where? Where are we going?'

Joel laughed and ushered them both to the car. 'If I told you that, it wouldn't be a mystery, would it? Hop in and you'll soon find out.'

He took them to the Sea Life Centre along the coast and Sam was almost speechless with awe when he saw the shark tank.

'Wow. That's so cool.'

Joel looked pleased with himself. 'I thought you'd like it. Aren't they amazing?'

Sam nodded vigorously. 'Would they eat you?'

'No, I don't think they're that type of shark. We can read about them if you like.' Joel strolled over to an information board and Sam joined him, reading it aloud.

Joel looked at him in surprise. 'You read well.'

Sam swelled with pride. 'My mum taught me. I could read when I was four.'

'Could you, now? You must have a pretty special mum.' Joel's eyes rested on Lucy and she blushed.

They spent an hour looking round the Sea Life Centre and then they walked down the road to find somewhere to eat.

'You know, pizza would be nice,' Lucy suggested, and Joel grinned.

'Great. Better than hamburger.'

They found a pizza restaurant, settled themselves at a table and Joel ordered the food.

Soon they were chatting about the sharks, Sam's school and Cornwall in general.

'I love it here, Mum. It's heaps better than where we

lived before. Imagine having sharks living so close.' Sam had his mouth full of pizza and was grinning from ear to ear. 'And with Joel here, it's almost like being a proper family again.'

Lucy felt as though she'd jumped naked into a freezing bath. 'We *are* a proper family, sweetheart,' she said, trying to hide her dismay at his comment.

Joel had stopped eating and was looking at Sam. 'Why does having me here make you feel like a proper family?' His voice was gruff and Sam stared at them miserably, obviously aware that he'd said something wrong.

'Because families usually have a daddy,' he mumbled. 'Kevin's mum and dad split up, but now he has another daddy. A different daddy. I think I'd like another daddy. You'd be a nice daddy.'

Lucy looked at him, appalled and embarrassed. 'Sam—'

'Hush, it's OK.' Joel reached across the table and grasped her hand, indicating that she should leave it to him. 'Why would you like to have another daddy, Sam?'

'Because it makes Mummy laugh,' Sam said immediately. 'When it's just the two of us, she's often sad. But when you're there she's always smiling.'

'Sam, please…' Lucy was mortified, and Joel tightened his grip on her hand.

'It must have been very hard on your mum, not having your dad around,' he told Sam quietly. 'It's not surprising she sometimes feels sad.'

'But she's not sad since she met you. So she should marry you,' Sam said firmly.

Joel's eyes met Lucy's and she looked away immediately, scarlet with embarrassment.

What had she done?

She should never have allowed her friendship with Joel to develop. It hadn't occurred to her that Sam might misinterpret their relationship. She'd never imagined that he was so desperate for a man's attention that he'd latch onto Joel as a prospective father.

'Joel is just a friend, Sam,' she said quickly, dragging her hand away from Joel's and wondering how such a happy afternoon could have suddenly turned so awful.

'But you don't cry any more,' Sam said, and Joel frowned.

'Did she used to cry?'

Sam nodded, exchanging a grown-up look with Joel. 'At night. When she thought I was asleep. But I could hear her through the wall.'

Lucy closed her eyes and wished she were somewhere else.

So much for putting on a brave face around her son. She'd never realised that the walls of their London flat had been so thin.

'I don't expect your mum really wants to think about getting married again at the moment,' Joel said, his tone matter-of-fact as he finished his pizza. 'Sometimes, if you've had a bad experience, it puts you off for a while, you know?'

Sam looked at him and nodded slowly. 'I suppose so.'

Lucy was staring at the remains of her pizza without seeing it.

'Don't worry, Mum.' Sam's voice was comforting. 'It's OK by me if you don't want to get married again yet. I'm just glad you're not crying any more.'

She cleared her throat and looked at her son, aged six going on sixty. 'Oh, good...I...er...'

'Finish your pizza, Sam, before it goes cold,' Joel suggested calmly, gesturing to the waiter and ordering more drinks.

But Lucy couldn't eat another thing. All she could think about was Sam. She hadn't realised that he felt like that.

They left the restaurant and drove home, Lucy protesting that they still needed to pick up her car from the surgery.

'I'll give you a lift in tomorrow,' Joel said, heading back for the flats.

Lucy barely said a word on the way home, her head clouded with worries and guilt.

Did Sam really miss having a daddy so much?

She'd tried so hard to make up for Tim leaving.

Was she really so miserable to be with?

'Lucy...' Joel's gentle voice interrupted her tortured thoughts and she looked at him blankly. 'We're home.'

She looked out of the window, realising that she hadn't even noticed the journey.

'Oh, Thank you.' She fumbled with the doorhandle, aware that Joel was frowning at her with concern. 'Come on, Sam. Time to do some reading and then bed. What do you say to Joel?'

'Thank you,' Sam recited obediently. 'But can't Joel come in and read my story?'

'No, absolutely not.' Lucy bustled him out of the car and up the stairs to her flat. 'Joel has heaps of other things to do. Say goodnight.'

'Goodnight, Joel.'

She couldn't bring herself to meet his eyes, still painfully embarrassed by the things that Sam had said, but she felt his hesitation.

'Goodnight.' He seemed about to say something else but then gave a little sigh. 'See you in the morning.'

And with that he turned on his heel and walked away, leaving mother and son together.

*   *   *

Joel sat in his penthouse, staring across the sparkling lights of the harbour. Normally the view helped him to relax, but tonight it was doing absolutely nothing for him.

He was too worried about Lucy.

She'd made it obvious that she'd wanted him to leave her and Sam alone together, and he understood that. After that heavy conversation at the table she had serious things to discuss with her son.

Sam.

He frowned, curious at how attached he'd become to the boy. And he loved Sam's honesty. Unlike Lucy, who'd clearly been mortified by his announcement that he wanted a father, Joel had been intrigued and moved. Dealing with adults was so much more complicated, he reflected. They rarely said exactly what they meant and you were left trying to read body language. But children just said what was bothering them…

He sighed and ran his fingers through his hair.

You didn't need to be a genius at reading adult body language to realise that Lucy had been horrified by Sam's comments. What had scared her the most? he wondered. The fact that Sam wanted her to marry again, or the fact that Sam wanted her to marry *him*?

If he hadn't been so worried about Lucy, he would have smiled. He'd been on the receiving end of plenty of match-making in his time, but never from a six-year-old boy.

But he *was* worried about Lucy. Especially worried about the amount that Sam said she cried.

It must have been incredibly hard for her, trying to hide her own emotions from Sam. The thought of her crying on her own in the bedroom at night made his insides twist into knots.

He glanced at his watch and saw that it was ten o'clock.

Sam would be asleep by now. And what would Lucy be doing?

Crying again?

Swearing softly, he stood up, picked up his keys and quietly let himself out of his apartment. He'd just check that she was all right, he told himself, otherwise he wouldn't be able to sleep.

Lucy took a long time to answer the door, and he was just about to give up, assuming that she'd gone to bed, when the door opened slowly and she stood there wearing a white fluffy dressing-gown, her hair damp and loose around her narrow shoulders.

He could see in an instant that he'd been right. Her pale face wore the evidence of recent tears, and he realised that there was no way he could go back to bed and leave her like that.

'Did you want something?' Her voice sounded slightly hoarse—another indication that she'd been crying.

'I wanted to check on you,' he said quietly, stepping forward into the flat even though he hadn't been invited. 'That was a very heavy chat we had over the pizza.'

'Yes.' She closed the door, tied her dressing-gown cord tighter and gave him a formal smile. All the closeness they'd achieved over the past few weeks seemed to have gone. 'I apologise for that. Please, don't let Sam's comments panic you. He's obviously just desperate for male company. I hadn't realised how desperate.'

She was obviously still feeling awkward about what Sam had said.

'He didn't panic me,' Joel said slowly, 'but he obviously upset you.'

'Well, it's not every day your six-year-old son proposes to a man for you.' Her brave attempt at a joke made his heart ache.

'Is that why you're so upset? Because you were embarrassed by what he said to me?'

She was silent for a long time. 'Partly,' she admitted finally. 'I suppose I was most upset that he's so desperate for a father. I thought I was doing so well, especially since we moved here. I thought I was giving him everything other families had. Clearly I was wrong.'

Joel frowned. 'Don't be so hard on yourself.'

'Why?' Her expression was bleak. 'I've obviously done a lousy job of hiding how upset I've been. The poor child will probably be scarred for ever by hearing me cry in my bedroom.'

'That's nonsense,' Joel said softly. 'Children are stronger than that.'

'I thought that coming to Cornwall would be a fresh start.'

'And have you cried in your bedroom since you arrived?'

She looked at him and shook her head. 'No.'

'Until tonight, you mean,' he pointed out with a wry smile.

'I feel like a really bad mother.' Her eyes filled and he ignored all the alarm bells sounding in his head and pulled her into his arms, folding her against his chest. He felt her feeble resistance but there was no way he was letting her go.

'You're a great mother Lucy,' he said gruffly, gritting his teeth as he felt her sob into his chest. Damn. He hated to see her cry. His arms tightened around her body. 'Do you really miss Sam's father that much?'

'No.' She shook her head and pulled away from him, wiping her eyes on her sleeve like a child. 'I thought I did. But I think what I really missed was the safeness of it all, you know? Being with someone who's always known you gives life a predictability. When that went I felt like a ship without a rudder. For ages I was afraid that I wouldn't be able to cope on my own. But I have, of course. And as for the way I feel about Tim—well, I suppose part of me can't forgive him for what he did to Sam.'

'Has he never been in touch with him?'

Lucy shook her head, her expression bleak. 'Not once. He said that it wouldn't be fair on Sam but I think that's nonsense. He just didn't want a child any more.'

'We've never talked much about Tim,' Joel said softly. 'Had you known him long before you married him?'

She gave a watery smile. 'You think that if I tell you the whole sordid story then I'll feel better?'

Joel shrugged helplessly. 'I don't know. Perhaps it's worth a try.'

Lucy looked at him and then walked over to the window and stared out into the darkness, her eyes fixed on the lights of the fishing boats. 'When we were children we were next-door neighbours. We played together all the time. I suppose you could say that we were inseparable.'

'So he was the boy next door?'

'Literally.' Lucy nodded and hugged the dressing-gown closer. 'Everyone assumed we'd marry and that's exactly what we did. As soon as we both finished training.'

'Training? What did he do?'

'He was a nurse, too, but we weren't at the same hospital.' She sniffed quietly and rummaged in her pocket for a tissue. 'So, anyway, we did as everyone expected and married, and then we had Sam almost straight away. And it was pretty hard because Tim didn't earn enough on a nurse's salary and I had to go back to work, too.'

'Were you happy?'

She turned to look at him, her expression considering. 'I thought I was, but now, looking back, I'm not so sure.

I'd known Tim for so long that it was impossible to imagine life without him. When he left my whole world fell apart, especially when I saw what it did to Sam.' She shook her head and looked at him blankly. 'Why did he have to do it that way? Why couldn't he just have sat me down in a civilised way and told me how he felt? At least then we could have prepared Sam together so that he didn't feel so rejected.'

'He seems like a pretty well-adjusted little boy to me,' Joel said quietly. 'I'd say you've done a damn good job bringing him up on your own. I didn't realise that you married the first man you met. Was he really your only relationship?'

She nodded slowly. 'Hard to believe, really, isn't it? Shall I tell you something funny?' She gave a short laugh and bit her lip. 'I've only ever kissed one man in my life. Just Tim. I've never even kissed anyone else. Can you imagine that?'

'Not really.' He shook his head and gave a faint smile. 'Weren't you ever curious as to how it would be with someone else?'

There was a long silence and he felt his pulse rate increase as her eyes locked with his.

'No…'

Something in her eyes told him that she was lying.

And suddenly he couldn't help himself. He walked across the room towards her, his eyes never leaving hers for a moment.

'You've never once wondered what it would feel like to be kissed by another man?'

Her lips parted and he saw her breathing quicken.

'Never, Lucy?'

He cupped her face in his hands, his eyes dropping to

her soft, pink mouth. He'd wanted to kiss her for so long, the tension was almost unbearable.

He lowered his head, waiting for her to pull away, but she didn't. She didn't speak at all. She just stood, immobile, her small hands clenched by her sides, her eyes trapped by his.

And then, incredibly gently, his mouth found hers.

Forcing himself to exercise restraint, he kept the strength of his desire firmly reined in, concentrating instead on exploring every millimetre of her mouth.

With a thrill of triumph he felt her hands creep slowly up to his chest and then slide tentatively around the back of his neck.

Still keeping one hand behind her head, he slid the other one down her back, pulling her gently against him, letting her feel what she did to him. He felt a shiver run through her body and knew that, whatever he was feeling, she was feeling it, too.

His hand slid over the full curve of her bottom and he deepened the kiss, knowing that he was fighting a losing battle with his will-power. He was fast discovering that he didn't want to hold back. He wanted to discover more of Lucy. He wanted everything she had to give.

But it was too soon, of course.

Realising that if he didn't stop torturing them both he'd be in trouble, Joel summoned up his flagging will-power and lifted his head.

Immediately her eyes opened and she dipped her head, her forehead resting gently on his chest.

Was she afraid to look at him?

'Lucy?' He tucked a finger under her chin and lifted her face so that she had to look at him. 'I know I'm supposed to say I'm sorry, but it would be a lie, and I won't lie to you—ever.'

She wriggled away from him, clearly embarrassed. 'Well, at least I know what it's like to kiss another man now.'

Her tone was light, but he could sense her confusion and he didn't know what to do about it.

'It was just a kiss Lucy,' he reassured her softly. 'It doesn't have to be any more than that if you don't want it to be.'

But he desperately hoped that she did want it to be something more.

CHAPTER SEVEN

LUCY stared at the peak-flow meter in her hand and tried to concentrate.

But all she could think of was what it had felt like to be kissed by Joel.

She still wasn't sure what had happened to her.

She'd been kissed by Tim a thousand times over the years they'd been together, and never, never even once, had it felt like that.

And if that was what kissing Joel could feel like, then what would it feel like to...?

She shook her head slightly, shocked by her own thoughts.

What on earth was happening to her?

She sat down on the chair in the treatment room with a plop, wondering suddenly if this was what Tim had felt. Was that why he'd left? Had he suddenly discovered a new, exciting feeling that the two of them had never experienced together?

Stunned by the direction of her thoughts, she lifted a hand to her mouth. Even after he'd left, she'd never questioned her feelings for Tim. She'd always been so sure that he was the only man for her. But she'd never felt one tenth of the excitement when Tim walked into a room that she experienced when she saw Joel.

So what did that mean? Had Tim been right all along when he'd said that they were wrong for each other? She tried to remember some of the things that he'd said in the letter he'd left on the kitchen table, but she'd been so devastated by his actions that she'd barely read further than the first line.

She looked up as the door opened and Ros walked into the room.

'Dear me, you look white as a sheet!' She was across the room in seconds, concern clearly visible on her face. 'Has something happened?'

Yes.

After Joel's kiss the night before, her whole world had been turned upside down. She'd always thought that there was no excuse for what Tim had done. And of course there was no excuse for the way he'd treated Sam. But as for their relationship—she was beginning to wonder whether there *was* more to a relationship than what she had shared with Tim.

'I'm fine, Ros,' she said quietly. 'Just a bit tired.'

And confused.

'I'm not surprised,' Ros said briskly. 'You're on your own with a child and you're working—it's no wonder you're tired. Sit there for a moment and I'm going to bring you a cup of tea.'

'My asthma clinic is about to start,' Lucy protested weakly, and Ros snorted.

'They can wait five minutes.'

She bustled out of the room and was back minutes later with a steaming mug of tea.

'Here, drink this.' She handed the mug to Lucy, who took it gratefully.

Aware that Ros was hovering, watching her like a mother hen, she drank the tea and felt instantly better.

'Thanks, Ros. You're a lifesaver.' She stood up and smiled. 'OK. Bring them on!'

Her first patient was Mrs Lambert, who was due for a routine check.

'I've been blowing into that funny little machine, just as you said,' she said briskly, delving in her bag for her chart. 'And so far, touch wood, I've been fine. I haven't even had one of my chests this winter.'

Lucy scanned the peak-flow readings carefully. 'Well, you had the flu jab, Mrs Lambert, and the pneumonia jab so those will have helped. And we increased the dose of your puffer.'

'I never had jabs before this winter.' Mrs Lambert sniffed. 'Frankly, I thought it was all a load of nonsense. But I was so ill last winter that Dr Richard gave me a telling-off. Bullied me into having them, he did.'

Lucy smiled, knowing full well that Annie Lambert adored Richard Whittaker.

'Well, they've made a difference, Mrs Lambert,' she said quietly, 'so perhaps it's just as well he bullied you. These readings are good. No problems, then?'

'None at all, but I do think this asthma thing is all nonsense. I've said it before and I'll say it again. I don't wheeze, for goodness' sake!'

'You don't necessarily have to wheeze,' Lucy told her. 'Small children with asthma don't always wheeze. Sometimes their only symptom is a cough. In older people the only symptom may be breathlessness.'

Mrs Lambert looked unconvinced. 'I'm seventy,' she reminded Lucy stoutly. 'I've never had asthma, or any other sort of illness come to that, until the last few years. How can I suddenly have asthma now?'

'Sometimes people are diagnosed with asthma for the first time later in life,' Lucy explained. 'And the reason that Dr Richard encouraged you to have the vaccinations is that in older people it can be triggered by flu, colds or other viral infections.'

'Well, I was certainly very breathless last winter, when

I had my awful chest,' Mrs Lambert told her. 'But I wasn't very co-operative when Dr Richard tried to start me on all sorts of inhalers.'

'Don't worry about that now.' Lucy gave her a warm smile and handed her chart back to her. 'All that matters is that you're doing really well, and you are.'

She talked to Mrs Lambert for a few more minutes and then called her next patient.

It was Margaret Patterson, who had returned for her repeat spirometry.

'I've stopped coughing now,' she told Lucy with a smile, 'so perhaps we'll have more success this time. I wrote down my peak-flow results, by the way.'

She handed the piece of paper to Lucy, who scanned it quickly.

'OK, I want to do the spirometry now.' She handed the machine to Margaret and this time she was able to blow without coughing.

'That's great.' Lucy recorded the results and then asked her to inhale a drug that would dilate her airways. 'The results we get after you've taken this drug will help us decide if it's COPD or asthma.'

But the results weren't what she'd been expecting, and later on that day she tracked down Joel, trying not to think about *that kiss*.

'Her spirometry showed a moderate airflow obstruction, but then I did reversibility testing with 5 mg salbutamol.' She showed Joel the results and he whistled with surprise.

'That degree of reversibility is suggestive of asthma.'

'But her serial peak flow readings suggested COPD.'

He grinned. 'Who ever said medicine is an exact science?'

Despite herself, she found herself responding to that smile. 'So now what?'

Joel inhaled deeply and gave it some thought. 'We give her a trial of high-dose inhaled steroids. I'll give her beclomethasone for six weeks. Get her to come back at the end of that time and we'll test her again. If her lung function is back within normal limits, we'll know that it's asthma, not COPD. Send her into me when you've finished with her.'

Lucy returned to her treatment room and explained the results of the tests to Margaret.

'So I need to see Dr Whittaker again?'

Lucy nodded. 'He'll give you a prescription. He's free now, so you can pop straight over to his room.'

She worked her way through to the end of her asthma clinic and then looked up as Joel walked into the room.

'What are you doing at lunchtime?'

She stared at him. 'H-having a sandwich, I suppose. Why?'

He grinned. 'Tina's just called me. She's just found a dress that she thinks is made for you.'

'A dress?' Her eyes widened. She'd completely forgotten about the Valentine's Ball. In fact, since he'd kissed her, she'd pretty much forgotten about everything.

'Don't look so surprised.' He looked at her keenly. 'Are you changing your mind about coming with me?'

He had a way of looking at her—as though she were the only woman in the world—and her heart beat faster.

'I'm still coming.'

'Good.' His voice was soft. 'I'm going to make sure you have a night to remember.'

She looked into his eyes and swallowed, wondering what he had in mind. Were they still just friends, or had that kiss moved the boundaries of their friendship? And did she want it to?

*   *   *

Tina's boutique was on the harbour front and Joel parked the car right outside.

'The advantages of the middle of winter,' he said with a laugh as he switched off the engine. 'In the summer season you can't even drive along this road, let alone park.'

Lucy tried to imagine the Cornish fishing village crammed with tourists, and failed. She wasn't sure she'd like it crowded. She was growing to love the shriek of the seagulls and the wildness of the winter sea.

Tina came to the door and smiled at them. 'I made coffee and I bought pasties from the Quay.'

Inside the tiny shop Lucy stopped and blinked. It was like Aladdin's cave. Brightly coloured dresses and jewellery were artfully arranged to catch the eye and intrigue the casual shopper.

'That's so pretty,' she murmured, fingering a pale pink top with delicate beading around the edges.

'Isn't it lovely?' Tina beamed at her and then propelled her through to the back room. 'But you don't want that. I've found something spectacular for you.'

Just then Joel's mobile rang and he rolled his eyes and finished his mouthful of pasty. 'No peace for the wicked.'

He answered the phone and listened, his expression suddenly serious. 'I'll be there.'

'Michael's been called to an emergency and there are patients piling up so I need to go back.' He picked up the rest of the pasty and dropped a kiss on Tina's cheek. 'Thanks for lunch. Can you be an angel and run Lucy back to the surgery when you've finished?'

Tina nodded and Joel turned to Lucy with an apologetic smile. 'Sorry to abandon you.'

'No problem.'

'Make sure she doesn't buy anything conservative' was Joel's parting shot as he sprinted out of the door to his car.

'Nothing conservative, eh?' Tina smiled at Lucy. 'He's going to love what I've chosen. Wait there.'

She emerged a few seconds later, carrying a long sheath of blue-green silk which she handed to Lucy. 'Try it. With your colouring it will look stunning.'

Lucy looked at it doubtfully. 'I've never worn anything that glamorous before.'

'All the more reason to start now,' Tina said firmly. 'Changing room is behind you.'

Not wanting to argue, Lucy walked into the changing room and slid out of her uniform, staring at the dress on the hanger. Would she ever dare wear it?

Well, there was no harm in trying it on, she reassured herself, reaching for the dress and stepping into it.

'Are you decent?' Tina's voice came from behind the curtain and Lucy gave a hollow laugh.

'It's impossible to be decent in this dress.'

Tina whipped back the curtain and frowned. 'You've left your bra on.'

Lucy looked at her, shocked. 'Well, of course I've left my bra on.'

Tina shook her head. 'That dress needs you to go bra-less.'

'Tina, I'm hardly small in that department,' Lucy pointed out, scarlet with embarrassment as Tina delved inside the dress and deftly removed her bra. 'I need to wear a bra.'

'Not with this dress you don't,' Tina said firmly, picking up a packet of pins and making some quick adjustments. 'There, that's better. Just scoop your hair up... Perfect.' She smiled with satisfaction. 'Now look at yourself.'

Lucy glanced at her reflection and her eyes widened. A

complete stranger stared back at her. The stranger had lush, extravagant curves and a ridiculously tiny waist.

Was it really her?

'You look sensational,' Tina said, an awed expression on her pretty face. 'I'd do anything for a figure like yours. That dress was made for you.'

Lucy tugged dubiously at the neckline. 'It's too revealing. And I'm too top-heavy.'

'Nonsense. It's totally stunning.' Tina stepped back and narrowed her eyes. 'Joel isn't going to be able to keep his hands off you.'

Remembering the previous night's kiss, Lucy felt a blush come to her cheeks and Tina gave a cheeky grin.

'Come on—tell me everything.'

'There's nothing to tell,' Lucy said firmly, but Tina's smile was so warm and understanding and she was such a kind person that Lucy found herself telling Tina everything.

'You married your childhood sweetheart? Wow.' Tina shook her head slowly as Lucy came to the end of her story. 'I mean, that's great,' she said, correcting herself hastily. 'I just can't imagine it myself. What happened when you were training? Did you do the usual round of drunken parties?'

Lucy shook her head. 'Not really. I was nineteen when we married, and we didn't go out much, to be honest.'

'Oh.' Tina looked taken aback and then gave a sheepish grin. 'In that case, remind me never to tell you about my university days. You'd be scandalised.'

Lucy smiled. 'I don't think so.'

Tina looked at her curiously. 'Didn't you ever feel that you missed out? While the rest of us were all experimenting, you were already married.'

'And raising a family,' Lucy said quietly. 'I had Sam when I was twenty.'

Tina nodded slowly and fingered the gorgeous dress. 'So now maybe it's time to have some fun, Lucy Bishop. You need to live a little. Think of enjoying yourself, and nothing else.'

'I have a child!'

Tina raised an eyebrow. 'And he's going to mind if his mother wears a stunning dress that makes her look like a film star? I don't think so.'

Lucy looked at her reflection and felt a thrill of excitement. She'd never worn a dress like this before, and suddenly she wanted to, more than anything in the world.

'I'll have it,' she said shyly, and Tina whooped.

'That's my girl! Let's knock him dead!'

As she prepared for her afternoon clinic, Lucy couldn't stop thinking about what Tina had said.

Had she really missed out? While everyone else had been partying, she and Tim had been building a home together. At the time she'd never even questioned what they were doing—it had just seemed to be the inevitable conclusion of their relationship.

But had they both misunderstood their relationship? Had she been too young and inexperienced to understand the difference between friendship and true love?

Was that why Tim had left?

Had he found something different with the young woman he'd left her for?

Puzzled and thoughtful, she worked her way through her afternoon list.

Her second patient was Penny, the girl she and Joel had seen a few weeks before.

Lucy greeted her and asked her how she was.

'Well, I had my period, so that was a good thing,' Penny said, clearly relieved that her one-night stand hadn't led to an unwanted pregnancy. 'I took the pills, like Dr Whittaker said, and I wasn't sick or anything.'

'Good.' Lucy looked at her expectantly and Penny blushed and fidgeted slightly in the chair.

'I'm sorry. I know I shouldn't have come back to you, but you were so kind to me and—' She broke off and Lucy gave her hand a squeeze.

'Just tell me what's worrying you.'

'Well, things don't feel right,' Penny muttered, 'ever since…well…'

'In what way haven't they been right?' Lucy's tone was warm and encouraging. 'Don't be embarrassed, Penny. Just tell me what's worrying you.'

Penny bit her lip and scraped her hair behind her ear. 'I've been bleeding.'

'Did you have a normal period after you took the emergency contraceptive that Dr Whittaker gave you?'

'Oh, yes.' Penny nodded. 'But since then I've been spotting a bit and it just feels—well, uncomfortable.'

'Do you have any discharge?'

Penny blushed fiercely and nodded. 'Yes.'

Lucy's voice was gentle. 'Dr Whittaker suggested that you go to the sexual health clinic at the hospital for some swabs—did you do that, Penny?'

Penny shook her head. 'No. I couldn't face it. I just felt too embarrassed.' She stared at the floor miserably. 'I suppose I was just hoping that everything would go away if I ignored it.'

'The problem is, Penny, that you may have caught an infection from the man you slept with,' she said quietly. 'The clinic is equipped to test for all sorts of things and give advice.'

'But what if someone sees me there?'

'People go there for all sorts of reasons,' Lucy told her. 'Family planning advice included. And the staff are sympathetic and experienced. They're used to dealing with problems just like yours. And it's all confidential, of course. In fact, it's one of the few places in the hospital where you can refer yourself. You can make your own appointment without a GP referral, and they don't even tell your GP your results unless you give permission. So it really is confidential.'

'But if my mum found out that I'd been there…' Penny sighed and looked totally dejected. 'Do I have to go?'

'Well, we can't force you,' Lucy said, her tone sympathetic, 'but it would be the right thing to do. I need to ask you something else, Penny. Have you had sex with anyone else since your one-night stand?'

Penny shook her head. 'No way! I'm never having sex again.'

Lucy gave her a sympathetic look. 'You feel like that now because you've had a fright,' she said softly, 'but you won't feel that way for ever. Maybe you started a bit young. You need to wait until you're ready, and then think carefully about contraception and make sure you use condoms. In the meantime, I'm going to take a swab for something called chlamydia.'

Penny looked blank. 'What's that?'

'It's the most common, treatable sexually transmitted disease,' Lucy told her. 'The problem is that, left untreated, it can cause something called pelvic inflammatory disease which can sometimes make you infertile. We certainly don't want that happening to you, so we need to do some tests and then treat you if necessary. It would also be sensible for me to take a routine smear test.'

She explained what she wanted Penny to do and then took a smear and an endocervical swab.

'The results should be back in about four days,' she told Penny, 'so why don't you give me a call and we can take it from there? But I think you should consider going to the sexual health clinic.'

Penny bit her lip and adjusted her clothing. 'But now you've done the tests…'

'I can only do some of the tests,' Lucy explained. 'It really would be best if you went to the experts, but have a think about it and we can talk about it when you call in for your results.'

'All right. Thanks, Sister.' Penny gathered up her things and left the room leaving Lucy feeling uneasy.

Wanting to talk about Penny's case, she checked that there were no patients waiting and went to find Joel.

He was in his room, talking to Michael, and broke off when he saw her.

'Problems?' He lifted a dark eyebrow and she shook her head, embarrassed that she'd interrupted them.

'Nothing urgent. Sorry.' She made to slip away but Joel caught her arm.

'It's OK. There's no need to dash off,' he said firmly. 'Michael and I were just gossiping. You're not interrupting anything.'

Michael grinned. 'In other words, he's telling me to go and get on with some work.' He saluted his brother and left the room.

Joel looked at her, his hand still closed tightly over her wrist. 'What's worrying you?'

'Penny,' she told him. 'She came back to see me.'

She explained what had happened and he frowned and released her.

'If she's got a discharge, she really ought to go to the

sexual health clinic. I did tell her that she needed to do that.'

'I know, but she's young, she feels guilty about having a one-night stand and she just wants it all to go away,' Lucy said softly. 'I'm afraid that she isn't going to go at all, so I tested her for chlamydia and took a smear.'

Joel shook his head, clearly concerned. 'But you know that co-infection with other sexually transmitted infections often occurs. She still needs to go to the clinic.'

'I know that.' Lucy defended her decision. 'But if she refuses to go, then surely we're better off at least testing her for what we can.'

Joel sighed and ran his hands through his hair. 'Has she slept with anyone else since?'

Lucy shook her head and he gave a wry smile. 'So at least we don't have to worry about contacts. I suppose that's something to be thankful for.' He breathed out and thought for a moment: 'All right, well, you know I'd be more comfortable if she had a full-infection screen from the clinic but as you say, if she won't go, we can't make her. Let's see what her results are and think again.'

Lucy bit her lip. 'Maybe I should have offered to go to the clinic with her—'

'Lucy, you can't do that!'

'She's just a child, Joel,' Lucy reminded him, 'and she's scared and embarrassed—'

'And you've got too much on your plate to go and hold her hand.' Joel shook his head. 'You've done everything you can, Lucy. At some point she needs to take responsibility for her own health.'

He stretched an arm across his desk to access his e-mail, and her eyes dropped to his broad shoulders. She knew how it felt to be held against that chest.

She tried to remember a time when she'd reacted to Tim the way that she reacted to Joel but she couldn't.

So what did that mean?

Joel glanced up from his computer and she met the full force of that intense, blue gaze.

It was like touching an electric fence.

For a moment they were both silent, and then she cleared her throat and backed towards the door, breaking the contact.

It was stupid even dreaming about what it would be like with Joel. She wasn't his type of woman. He was used to smart, sophisticated types with a PhD in flirting. She had absolutely no idea how to flirt. Despite her marriage, she was far too inexperienced and naïve for a man like Joel.

And even a stunning dress wasn't going to change that.

Forcing her mind back to work, she returned to the treatment room and discovered that Ros had found her more patients. It was approaching three o'clock and she'd just seen the last one when Ros hurried into the room, her expression serious.

'We've just had a call from one of Ivy Williams's neighbours. She's had an accident.' Ros put a hand on Lucy's arm. 'I'm just preparing you, pet, because I know you're fond of her.'

'What's happened?'

Ros sighed. 'She was going to the shop for a few things and she was hit by a car. Someone said she didn't seem to look at all before she crossed the road. It was as if her mind was totally elsewhere.'

Lucy stared at her in horror. She knew exactly where Ivy's mind would have been. With her Bert.

'Is she—is she…?' Lucy couldn't even bring herself to ask the question but Ros read her mind.

'We've called an ambulance and I sent Joel, because

obviously he's more experienced in this sort of thing than anyone else. But I don't know how bad it is, I'm afraid. I just thought you ought to know.'

'Yes.' Lucy nodded. 'Thanks, Ros. I'm going home now anyway, so will you call me when you hear something?'

She could have called Joel's mobile, of course, but if he was battling to save Ivy she didn't want to disturb him.

She collected Sam from school and took him straight home, along with a friend whose mother had been asked to work a few extra hours. Lucy was only too pleased to help, knowing that the favour would be returned at some point in the future. That was how working mothers survived, by supporting each other in times of need. It was all about sisterhood.

Functioning on automatic, Lucy cooked sausages and mash, wondering whether Joel would have eaten. She hadn't heard anything from Ros and she didn't like to call because she knew that someone would phone her when they found a minute to do so.

But she couldn't concentrate on anything, and by the time she heard a tap on the door at eight o'clock she was completely on edge.

It was Joel, looking tense and exhausted, the beginnings of dark stubble darkening his jaw.

'Hi.'

She'd never seen him look tired or stressed before, but tonight he was showing signs of both and she opened the door immediately, worried about him. 'Come in. I've been waiting for some news, but I didn't want to call you in case I disturbed you.'

He followed her into the flat, his mouth a grim line. 'The news isn't good, I'm afraid.' He looked at her warily and she knew instantly.

'She's dead, isn't she?' Her voice was quiet and he nodded slowly.

'I'm sorry. I know you were fond of her. She really
didn't stand a chance. A woman who witnessed the accident said that she just stepped out into the road, almost as
if she didn't care what happened to her.'

'I don't think she did,' Lucy said softly. 'She hasn't
cared about anything since Bert died.'

Joel sighed. 'She had massive injuries. We did get her
to hospital and we did our best but, frankly, there was
never really a moment when we thought she'd survive.'

'Poor Ivy.' Lucy was troubled. 'Do you think she did it
on purpose? Maybe she was suicidal, and I didn't notice.'

Joel frowned and shook his head. 'No, don't think like
that. You were great. Dad told me that you visited her just
to check on her. The witness said she just looked as though
her mind was elsewhere.'

'With Bert,' Lucy said sadly. 'She was totally lost without him.'

Joel looked at her and then walked towards the window,
his expression unreadable. 'I can't imagine it,' he said quietly. 'I can't imagine loving anyone so much that without
them your own life seems pointless and empty.'

Lucy swallowed. 'Haven't you ever been in love?'

She knew that Joel had never been short of girlfriends.
Surely he'd cared about some of them?

'No.' He shook his head slowly. 'Never.' He gave a wry
smile and shrugged his broad shoulders. 'At least, I don't
think I have. What is love? I'm damned if I know, Lucy.'

For a moment his expression was bleak and then he
sighed. 'Why don't you tell me what it feels like to be in
love? Presumably you were in love with Tim when you
married him. Tell me how it felt.'

The crazy thing was, she couldn't remember. She

couldn't remember any of the things that Tim had made her feel.

She wasn't even sure if she'd really loved him.

She shook her head slightly, suddenly feeling strange. *When had it happened?*

When had she suddenly started to question the way she'd felt about Tim?

Joel was still looking at her. 'When did you know that Tim was the man you wanted to marry?'

Lucy opened her mouth, hesitating before she answered. 'I suppose everyone just assumed we would,' she said finally. 'Getting married just seemed like a natural progression to our friendship.'

Joel frowned. 'I'm no expert, but that doesn't sound like love to me. It sounds like convenience.'

Lucy gave a half-smile. 'But love isn't like the fairytales, Joel.'

'Isn't it?' Joel gave her a strange look. 'Actually, I've always assumed that it should be, if it's right. From the outside, looking in, my parents seem to have it, and Michael and Maria, and Nick and Tina. You only have to watch them together to see that they share something special. Something that is just between the two of them. Is that what you had with Tim?'

'I don't think so,' she said honestly. 'I just don't know how I felt about Tim any more. Everything is so mixed up. Anger at the way he left us and hurt Sam, fear of being on my own, loneliness—sometimes my emotions are in such a mess that I couldn't begin to untangle them.' She slipped her fingers into the pocket of her jeans and pulled out a crumpled letter. 'Do you know what I did tonight?'

'What?'

'I read Tim's letter for the first time. He left it on the table the day he decided to walk out.'

Joel looked astonished. 'And you'd never read it before?'

'Oh, I read it.' Lucy stared down at the paper, realising that looking at it didn't hurt any more. 'I read it, but I didn't *read* it, if you see what I mean.'

Joel shook his head and gave her an apologetic look. 'Frankly, no.'

Lucy gave a tiny smile. 'Well, I read the words, of course, but I didn't really try and understand or listen to what he was telling me in the letter. I was so angry and hurt by the way he'd behaved towards us that I couldn't see further than the obvious fact. That he'd left us.'

'But now?'

'Now I'm starting to wonder whether he was right.' She shook her head slightly. 'Not in the way he did it, of course—leaving Sam like that was unforgivable. But he said that we married for all the wrong reasons and maybe he was right.'

He stared at her. 'What made you decide all this?'

'I don't know.'

But she did know.

It was because of Joel.

Spending time with Joel had made her realise that what she'd had with Tim hadn't been right.

Suddenly she knew exactly what being in love felt like.

It was the way she felt about Joel.

Not that she'd ever tell Joel that, of course. He was probably used to women falling in love with him, but she certainly didn't want to admit that she'd joined their ranks. At least this way she'd keep him as a friend.

And that was all he would ever be, of course. Joel didn't know what love was. Which meant that he certainly wasn't in love with her.

'How do you know that someone is right, Lucy?' He

shrugged his shoulders helplessly. 'I'm so afraid I'll get it wrong.'

She smiled softly, thinking enviously of the woman Joel finally fell in love with. 'I suppose, when it happens, you'll just know. You just haven't met the right person, Joel.'

'Maybe not.' He gave a smile and reached out a hand. 'I've had a lousy day. I need a hug.'

She went willingly into his arms, and he folded her against him.

'I could get to like this friendship business,' he muttered into her hair, and she reflected on the irony of the situation.

At the beginning she'd only wanted friendship and Joel hadn't been sure that he could deliver, and now, when she was beginning to think she'd like their relationship to develop into something more, he was enjoying their friendship.

She leaned her head against his broad chest and closed her eyes, thinking of Tim and of Ivy.

'You know something?' Her voice was quiet and slightly muffled by the wool of his jumper. 'Despite the sadness of her death, I think that Ivy was lucky in many ways. She met the man of her dreams. So many people don't meet that person, or they meet them at the wrong time, or they meet them and the feeling isn't returned. I think Ivy was lucky, don't you?'

Joel's grip tightened and she felt his strong fingers under her chin, lifting her face to his.

'Maybe.' He stared down at her with a strange look in his eyes. 'Maybe she was.'

CHAPTER EIGHT

JOEL sat in the practice meeting and tried to concentrate on what his brothers were saying.

'Joel!' Michael's voice barked at him. 'You're away with the fairies, man! What's the matter with you today?'

Joel took a deep breath, wondering what they'd say if he confessed that he'd been thinking about love. Part of him wanted to know how his brothers had known they were in love, but it wasn't a question he'd ever dare ask. Anyway, he knew well enough that what was true for one person might not be true for another.

All he knew was that he was struggling with his relationship with Lucy. She'd asked for friendship and he was pretty proud of the way he'd behaved. Mostly—apart from that one lapse when he'd given way to his instincts and kissed her senseless—he'd kept his true feelings for her well under control.

But what were his true feelings for her?

He tried to concentrate on what Michael was saying about prescribing costs but his mind kept wandering back to Lucy. He found her attractive, of course, that was easy enough to identify, and normally he'd just have enjoyed the relationship until it was time to move on. That was what he'd always done in the past.

But Lucy was different.

For a start, she'd only ever been to bed with one man, which virtually made her a virgin as far as he was concerned. And then there was the fact that she just wasn't the type to have casual relationships.

But what else could he offer her?

He certainly wasn't in love with her.

Or was he?

Trying to analyse his feelings, he thought back to how he'd reacted to other women. He'd certainly never felt as protective towards anyone as he did towards Lucy. He stared at his notepad without seeing it. And he certainly hadn't subdued his own feelings before in order to be friends with a woman.

Maybe that was it. It was a purely physical thing. He was just frustrated.

One night with Lucy and all these confused feelings would go away.

'Why don't you go home, Joel?'

He jumped and realised that his father was talking to him. 'We're trying to run a meeting here and you're miles away.'

'Sorry folks.' He smiled apologetically. 'I've a few things on my mind.'

'We were talking about the Valentine's Ball.' His father looked at the agenda with the list of things to discuss. 'Michael will be on call. Is that still OK, Michael?'

Michael sighed. 'It's fine. Someone else can do it next year. Maria will be babysitting Sam, so I'll join her until I get called out.'

Joel smiled. 'Thanks, Mike.'

Michael scowled. 'You just be careful, baby brother.'

Joel nodded, knowing that Michael was talking about Lucy. He *was* being careful. Every time he felt like kissing her again he made himself scarce and took cold showers. And as for the ball, well how much trouble could he get into on the dance floor in front of his mother?

*   *   *

The evening of the Valentine's Ball was crisp and clear, and Lucy's insides churned with excitement as she dressed for the ball.

Tina had brought her own dress to the flat so that they could change together, and they stood in the bathroom, fiddling with make-up and giggling like teenagers.

'This reminds me of my college days.' Tina laughed, wincing as she poked herself in the eye with a mascara wand. 'Ouch. Do you want me to put your hair up for you?'

'Would you?' Lucy looked at her gratefully, knowing that she would never manage to create the look that Tina could. She was very gifted.

Satisfied with her own make-up, Tina sat Lucy in a chair and flicked open her bag. 'Right... Now, then...' She stared into the bag and then picked up a pair of scissors.

Lucy's eyes widened with alarm and Tina grinned.

'Trust me. I just want to trim the front bits. It will look better, I promise. You'll be able to peep out through these floaty strands. Very sexy and alluring.'

Alluring? Lucy looked at her doubtfully. She didn't have the first clue how to look alluring.

Tina snipped quickly and then pulled out a brush and clips and twisted Lucy's hair into a knot on the back of her head, teasing a few strands over her cheeks.

'Oh, perfect—no, you can't look yet.' Tina reached for her make-up box and picked out a few things. 'Just a touch of this... There—fantastic.'

She worked for another ten minutes and finally she straightened with a smile of satisfaction and reached for the dress.

'Time to go to the ball, Cinderella.'

Lucy slithered into the dress and Tina helped her fasten it.

'Perfect. Now look at yourself in the mirror.'

But before Lucy had a chance there was a loud banging on the door and Tina looked at her in dismay.

'They're here already? Where did the time go?'

She leaned forward and kissed Lucy on the cheek, giving her a saucy wink. 'Don't forget, tonight you're living those college years. *Go for it, girl!*'

With that she shimmied across the room, veiled her eyes in a sexy expression and opened the door.

Nick stood there, resplendent in a dinner jacket, and Tina sighed dramatically

'My hero.'

Nick glanced down at her cleavage and gave her a suggestive wink. 'Do we have to go to the ball?'

'Yes, we do.' Tina pretended to look shocked but she stood on tiptoe to kiss her husband. 'Have you warmed the car up for us?'

'We've booked a taxi so that we can drink. His engine and his meter are running as we speak, so get a move on. Is Lucy ready?'

Lucy stepped forward shyly, clutching the wrap that went with the dress. 'I'm here.'

Nick stared at her in silence and then cleared his throat and stepped to one side.

Joel walked past his brother and Lucy's breath caught as she looked at him. Dressed in a dark dinner jacket and bow-tie, he looked stunningly handsome.

'I— Hi…' Suddenly she felt hideously self-conscious, aware that he was looking at her differently.

'You look gorgeous.' His voice was husky and very male, and Tina gave a delighted smile.

'Isn't she beautiful?'

'Tina, please…' Lucy interrupted her, thoroughly embarrassed, but Joel was nodding slowly.

'Really beautiful.'

Nick was frowning. 'Joel...'

Joel tossed him a warning glance which Lucy didn't understand. Why was Nick looking at Joel like that?

Joel held out his arm, his eyes warm as he looked down at her. 'Come on then. Let's go and dance.'

He was as good as his word, and as soon as the meal and the speeches were over, he swept her onto the dance floor without listening to her arguments that she couldn't be the first person to dance.

To add to her embarrassment, as they walked onto the floor he reached up and tugged the pins out of her hair so that it tumbled loose and soft around her shoulders.

She gave a gasp of astonishment and touched her hair self-consciously. 'What are you doing?'

He grinned and shrugged. 'Sorry, but you look better with long hair.'

'But Tina thought—'

'Tina's not a man.' His slow, sexy smile lit a fire inside her and she felt a liquid warmth spread through her veins.

The jazz band was playing and he spun her onto the dance floor, never letting go of her for one second. He was a superb dancer, holding her close one minute, whirling her round the next, but always in control so that she completely forgot to feel embarrassed.

And she had fun.

More fun than she could remember having in years.

Maybe ever...

They danced without stopping for at least an hour, but finally the music slowed and he slid an arm round her and pulled her against him.

She felt the hard strength of his body pressing through the thin fabric of her dress and she gave a shiver of reaction. It was exciting and frightening at the same time, the way she felt when Joel touched her.

They would have danced for ever but Nick intervened, giving his brother a meaningful look as he pushed him to one side and pulled Lucy into his arms.

'Is something the matter?' Trying not to show her disappointment, Lucy looked up at him, wondering why he seemed so tense. He seemed angry with Joel, but what possible reason could he have for being angry?

She remembered the look that Nick had given Joel back at the apartment, and wondered what was going on.

'Nothing's the matter.' He gave her a reassuring smile and then sighed. 'Look, Lucy, I'm going to be honest...' His voice was hesitant. 'We're all worried about you.'

She stopped dead, no longer moving in time to the music as she looked up at him. 'Worried about me? Why?'

Why on earth were they worried about her? She actually felt better than she had for a very long time.

'We're all worried that you'll fall for Joel,' Nick said gently, his arms tightening around her. 'He's a great guy, and I love him, but he's never committed to a woman in his life and he'll break your heart.'

It was like being showered with cold water. Oh, Nick was right, of course. He wasn't telling her anything she didn't already know but, still, hearing him say it—*and tonight of all nights when she'd been having such a good time*—really hurt.

'W-we're just friends, Nick,' she stammered, and Nick looked her straight in the eye.

'Sweetheart, you are like an open book,' he said quietly. 'You adore him, Lucy. It's written all over your face.'

She stared at him, appalled, and then pulled herself together. 'D-does he know?'

Nick shrugged and then shook his head. 'I don't know—

I don't think so. He seems to have a lot on his mind at the moment, for some reason, so he's not himself. I just don't want him to take advantage of you.'

Lucy thought of all the long hours she and Joel had talked into the night—plenty of time for him to have taken advantage of her if that was all he was interested in.

But he hadn't done that.

Apart from that one spectacular kiss, he'd never touched her. Instead, he'd just been the friend he'd promised he'd be. And her happiness over the weeks since she'd met him had been entirely because of him.

'He hasn't taken advantage of me,' she said bleakly. 'And I'm not a child, Nick. I'm touched by your concern but you don't have to worry about me. Is that why you've been glaring at poor Joel? Because you're afraid he'll make a pass at me?'

Nick looked sheepish. 'We've been warning him off you from day one. Trust me, Lucy. You don't need Joel.'

Didn't she?

Oh, she knew that he wasn't the sort of man to offer her anything long term—but at least he was honest about that.

In fact, Joel had never been anything but honest. He'd even admitted that he had no experience in being just a friend. And he'd turned out to be the best friend she'd ever had.

And his honesty was part of the attraction. With Joel you knew exactly what you were getting.

She looked up at Nick, her thoughts clearer than they'd been for a long time.

She did need Joel. If only to help her find parts of herself that she'd never discovered before.

'I know you're trying to help, and you've all been really

kind, but I'm not made of glass.' She gave a slight smile and Nick shook his head regretfully.

'If you go after Joel, all you'll get is a short-term relationship, Lucy. Just as long as you realise that.'

'I realise that.'

But it was what she wanted.

She knew that now.

Tim hadn't been right for her, but she hadn't even known that because her experience of life had been so narrow.

It hadn't been until she'd met Joel that she'd realised just how complicated emotions could be. Tim had never unleashed any of the passion that she felt for Joel.

And she felt like a teenager—desperate to know what it would be like to—to…

She blushed at the thought of it, hoping that Nick couldn't read her thoughts. He obviously thought she was some sort of innocent creature who had to be protected from his brother's wicked ways.

But she didn't want to be protected.

She wanted to have an affair. A wild, uncomplicated physical affair. Something she'd never done before. Something she'd never dreamed of doing until she'd met Joel. And if it turned out to be very short-lived, well, she'd cope. She'd managed to cope with the fallout from Tim's actions so she could cope with anything.

Suddenly she felt stronger than she ever had before. And she felt proud of herself.

She *had* coped. She and Sam together. And she'd discovered things about herself that she hadn't even known before.

Like the fact that she'd rather have one night with the man she loved than a lifetime with someone that she didn't.

Wasn't that what Ivy had said? And she'd been right.

Suddenly she wanted Joel to take her home.

But what if he didn't want what she wanted?

As he strolled towards her over the dance floor she looked at him, long-limbed and drop-dead handsome, and suddenly doubted herself. Why would Joel, who was used to sophisticated, experienced women, want her?

With a last regretful look, Nick released her to his brother, but not before he'd said something under his breath that made Joel's shoulders tense.

'Don't tell me.' Lucy's voice was calm as he took her into his arms. 'He's just warned you that if you lay a finger on me he'll beat you to a pulp.'

Joel looked startled and then grinned. 'How did you guess?'

'Because he's just spent two whole dances lecturing me,' Lucy told him, smiling shyly. 'Apparently you're a real threat to my virtue.'

Joel smiled, and she noticed every detail of that smile. Like the way his eyes creased at the corners and a small dimple appeared at the side of his firm mouth.

'I think my self-control has been commendable,' he said quietly, his voice barely audible above the music, 'when I think what I've wanted to do to you.'

She could hardly breathe. 'Tell me what you've wanted to do.'

Neither of them were moving now. Instead, they stood in the centre of the dance floor, oblivious of the other dancers around them.

'I've wanted to make love with you since the first moment I saw you at the accident,' he said simply, his eyes steady on hers. He didn't look away for a moment, didn't make any apology for the way he felt. 'There's been a strong chemistry between us right from the start, Lucy, but you were so damned wary after what happened with Tim that you weren't having any of it. So I agreed to settle for friendship.'

She swallowed, her gaze captured by the tiny pulse working in his throat. 'And you've been the best friend I've ever had.'

'I don't think so.' He rubbed a hand over the back of his neck to relieve the tension. 'I think I've been a pretty lousy friend, Lucy.'

'Why do you say that?'

His hand dropped to his side. 'Because there's never been a moment when I haven't wanted you, and not dragging you into my arms and kissing you has been the biggest test of my life.'

'You did kiss me.'

'I don't need reminding,' he said quietly. 'Since that night I haven't slept much and my concentration at work has gone up the spout. I'm amazed my brothers haven't noticed.'

'They've noticed,' Lucy told him, remembering Nick's comments. 'But I don't think they realise that it's because of me.'

'Just as well.' He gave a wry smile. 'Or they'd definitely beat me to a pulp.'

Lucy looked up at him shyly. 'So—er—what are we going to do?'

'About what?'

'About the way you feel,' she murmured, her eyes dropping to his mouth and then lifting again to his eyes.

He licked his lips. 'Well...' He cleared his throat.' Nothing, I suppose. We carry on as friends.'

She nodded slowly, placing one small hand on the middle of his broad chest. 'If that's what you want.'

There was a long pause and then his fingers tightened

around her wrist and he lifted her face to his with his free hand.

'What do you mean? If that's what I want. This isn't about what *I* want. It's about what *you* want, and you just want us to be friends.'

She looked into his eyes, suddenly not knowing what to say. She'd never propositioned a man in her life before. How did she tell Joel she really wanted him to make love to her without looking like some sort of hussy?

Pink and embarrassed, she tried to dip her head, but there was no way he was letting her go.

'Lucy…?' His voice was a long, slow question and she blushed deeply.

'I—don't know, Joel…' She was stammering now. 'It's just that you make me feel… And I thought that I just wanted to be friends, but I'm—it's— Oh, help.'

She broke off and buried her face in his chest and felt him shaking with laughter.

'I don't understand a word you're trying to say,' he murmured in her ear, 'but I have a feeling that this isn't a conversation we should be having in a public place. Am I right?'

She nodded and he released her immediately, closing his long fingers around her wrist and leading her firmly away from the dance floor.

He led her outside, picking up their coats on the way, and flagged down a taxi that was hovering by the door.

'But we didn't even say goodbye to people,' she said breathlessly, as she scooped the hem of her long dress into the cab.

'You want me to be beaten to a pulp by my family?' Joel grinned at her. 'I'm fully expecting them to be hot on our heels, ready to break the door down and rescue you, any minute.'

She chuckled and looked away, suddenly terrified by what she was doing.

Did she really want just one night with Joel?

Well, no, of course she didn't, she reasoned. She wanted every night for the rest of her life, but that wasn't on offer so she'd take whatever she could get. She might not have much experience, but she'd seen enough of life to know that true love didn't come along very often, and when it did you had to grab it with both hands, even if it was only fleeting.

They were silent for the rest of the journey home, and all she could think about was the warm touch of his hand as he held hers firmly.

He paid the taxi driver, ushered her up to her apartment and waited while she opened the door.

Sam was staying the night with Michael and Maria so there was no fear of him disturbing them.

She'd been surprised and delighted by how excited Sam had been by the prospect of a night away from her, and she reflected on how much he'd improved since coming to Cornwall. He was growing into a secure, confident little boy and the invitation to 'camp' at Michael's and Maria's house had seemed like a huge adventure.

Which left her alone with Joel.

'Would you like a coffee?' Her fingers were shaking while she dealt with the lock, and he shook his head slowly.

'Not coffee,' he said, pushing her gently inside the flat and closing the door behind them. 'After dancing with you for most of the night, what I need most is a cold shower. And don't blush. You've been pressed up against me for long enough to know that I'm suffering from a serious case of frustration. What were you trying to tell me on the dance floor, Lucy?'

He hadn't bothered to turn on the hall light and they were in semi-darkness. Suddenly the intimacy of her flat made her all the more aware of just how daring she'd been.

She stood with her back to the wall and he placed an arm on either side of her head so that she couldn't avoid him.

'You were saying that you thought you just wanted to be friends,' he prompted her gently, 'and then you paused. So what are you saying, Lucy?'

She didn't know what to say to him, so instead she stood on tiptoe and kissed him gently.

He stiffened and stayed immobile, and then he gave a groan and took over, his mouth dominating and devouring hers in a kiss that had nothing whatsoever to do with friendship.

Whereas their first kiss had been gentle and exploratory, this one was hot and demanding, and he took everything she was willing to give.

His body pressed hers against the wall and she felt the hard ridge of his arousal through the thin silk of her dress.

A totally unfamiliar feeling curled through her body, a fiery, sexual heat which consumed every last doubt she might have had.

Hardly aware of what she was doing, she reached inside his jacket and tugged at his shirt, giving herself access to his warm, muscular body.

As her fingers touched his heated flesh she gave a shiver of anticipation. He felt so strong, so vitally masculine...

As his kiss became more intimate, so did his hands, and she only realised that he'd unzipped her dress when she felt cool air brush her skin as the dress slipped down and pooled on the floor by her feet. The touch of his fingers on her breasts made her gasp into his mouth and she reached for the buckle of this trousers, too far gone to be shocked by her own actions.

His fingers closed over her wrist in an iron grip and finally he lifted his head, his breathing unsteady and his eyes dark with desire.

'Lucy…' His voice cracked and he cleared his throat and dropped his head onto his forearm while he tried to regain some semblance of self-control. 'I need…' He lifted his head and looked into her eyes. 'I need to know this is what you want, sweetheart. Because if you want me to stop, it has to be now.'

Lucy looked at him, her whole body aching with a desire she hadn't known it was possible to feel.

She was well aware of the enormity of what she was about to do, but there was no way she wanted to stop.

'I don't want you to stop, Joel.'

He closed his eyes briefly. 'Are you sure?'

She nodded slowly. 'Completely sure. I want you to make love to me, Joel—please?'

But still he didn't move, his expression tormented, as if he was fighting some sort of internal battle.

'What's wrong?' She touched his face with gentle fingers and he dropped a kiss onto her hand.

'I—I just want to make sure you understand—'

'That you're not the sort of man who makes a commitment,' she said quietly, reading his mind. 'I know that, Joel. I know exactly how you feel. We've been friends long enough for me to have understood that. I know what you're offering, Joel. Uncomplicated sex.'

He winced slightly and she gave a gentle smile and stood on tiptoe to kiss his mouth.

'It's OK. It's what I want.'

'You're sure?'

She nodded and blushed. 'It feels a bit scary, though.'

'No.' He shook his head and took her hand, leading her through to the sitting room. 'Don't be scared.'

'I can't help it.' She turned to face him, shaking slightly in a mixture of nerves and excitement. 'I've never done this before—you know that...'

'Don't be scared,' he repeated softly, his warm fingers sliding underneath the elastic of her panties as he dispensed with the last of her clothing.

Suddenly she was naked and she stood still, nibbling her lip, transfixed by the look in his eyes.

'Has anyone ever told you you're stunning?' With a fractured groan he bent his head and kissed her again, his mouth caressing and seducing hers, hinting at the intensity of what was to come.

Without lifting his head, he shrugged off his jacket and let it drop onto the floor, then tugged at his bow-tie.

The delicious torture of his mouth on hers was too much for her and she lifted her hands and tried to hurry him, tearing at his buttons in her hurry to free him of his shirt.

Finally the buttons were undone and she slid her fingers into the rough hair on his chest, feeling a thrill of excitement stab deep inside her.

Still kissing her, he let his fingers slide to the button of his trousers, but she was there before him, feeling the swollen ridge of his erection brush against her hand.

Finally he was naked as well, and she pulled her mouth away from his, looking at him shyly.

'You don't have to be afraid to look, Lucy,' he said hoarsely, 'It's OK to look.'

He was his usual confident self, completely unselfconscious about his own nudity. And why should he be? He had a fantastic body. Muscular, firm and athletic in all the right places, and as for the other places...

She looked down at him and he muttered something

under his breath and kissed her again, this time tucking one leg behind hers and pulling her gently off balance so that she ended up on her back on the huge soft rug in front of the fire.

The touch of his mouth on her breast made her gasp and she arched her back, moaning as darts of sensation spread down through her body, making her twist against him.

She was desperate for more—for everything—desperate for him to touch her there…

But he didn't. At least, not immediately.

Instead, he took his time, exploring every inch of her quivering, heated body with gentle strokes of his very clever tongue.

Finally, when she could bear it no longer, he moved over her, his eyes locking with hers as he parted her thighs.

'I have never,' he said slowly, 'wanted a woman the way I want you.'

And he bent his head to kiss her again, slowly and deliberately stoking the heat between them until she was almost begging him to finish what he'd started.

He entered her with a smooth thrust and she cried out as she felt his silken fullness deep inside her.

'Look at me, Lucy.'

Her eyes flew to his and he caught her hands and lifted her arms above her head, as if he was determined to join every part of them.

The raw intensity of his gaze burned through to her soul, but he wouldn't let her look away, wouldn't let her deny what was happening between them.

And it was like nothing she'd ever felt before. She knew now that whatever she had felt with Tim, it had never been like this. Never come near to this earth-shaking, overwhelming build of pleasure that threatened to consume every inch of her.

Knowing exactly how to make her body respond to him, Joel changed the angle slightly, a faint sheen of sweat on his brow as he created a rhythm so exquisite that it was almost unbearable.

There was something unbelievably erotic about the way that he kept eye contact as he moved deeply inside her, and Lucy clung to him, not understanding what was happening to her. It wasn't just her body he was controlling, it was her emotions.

Even as she felt her body reach its peak, he wouldn't let her look away, his eyes still on hers as they both reached an electrifying climax that swept them both along in its path.

CHAPTER NINE

IT WAS the doorbell that woke them.

Startled, Lucy sat upright, scrabbled around on the floor for her watch and gave a gasp.

'Oh, no! Joel, wake up!' She gave him a gentle shake, trying not to look at the sleek muscles of his shoulders. It was over. She'd had her night of passion and now it was time to return to the reality of her life.

Sam.

She scooped up her dress and all the other evidence, sprinted to her bedroom to hide it and grabbed her dressing-gown. In the meantime, Joel had pulled on his trousers and shirt and given her a sleepy, sexy smile.

'Oops!' He hadn't woken up properly and his voice was gruff and masculine. She felt her heart turn over with love. She wanted to savour what they'd had, to relive every incredible minute, but the hour was past and there was no time for such self-indulgence.

'I'll take them into the kitchen and you can make your escape.'

He frowned slightly and his hand closed over her wrist, preventing her escape. 'Lucy, wait—'

'Joel, we've got to let them in.' Her voice was an urgent whisper and she couldn't meet his eyes. She wasn't used to morning-after chat. It wasn't something she'd ever done before. Maybe Sam's early arrival was a good thing. It stopped her having to hear Joel tell her that last night had just been a one-off experience.

'Dammit, Lucy, look at me.' His voice was a husky growl and he dragged her towards him. 'We need to talk.'

'There's nothing to talk about,' she muttered, and he swore under his breath.

'Oh, yes, there is. Last night.'

'Oh, come on, Joel.' She fixed a brave smile on her face. 'We both know that last night was just a one-off. We agreed that before we did it. No commitment, remember?'

The doorbell rang again and he made an impatient sound, his fingers tightening around her wrist.

'Lucy—'

Summoning up all her will-power, she stood on tiptoe and kissed his cheek, feeling the rough stubble under her lips.

'Last night was amazing, Joel. I'll never forget it. You've shown me that there's plenty of things in life left for me to discover.'

Without waiting for him to answer, she walked towards the front door, leaving him no choice but to walk towards the bedroom.

Lucy took a deep breath and opened the door.

Tina stood there, with Sam by her side, and Lucy looked at her in surprise.

'Oh—I thought Maria was coming.'

Tina gave her a knowing grin. 'I thought maybe I'd better come. I wasn't sure—er…' She broke off and glanced over Lucy's shoulder into the flat. 'Well, anyway, I said I needed to collect my dress.'

Lucy stooped to hug Sam, who was full of excitement about his night with Michael and Maria.

'Guess what, they let me sleep on a camp bed in their room.' Sam's eyes were almost popping out as he regaled her with the details. 'It was great, Mum. Michael says when the weather is warmer, maybe we can go camping properly.'

'What a great idea.' Lucy smiled at her son and turned to Tina. 'Coffee?'

'As long as I'm not interrupting anything.' Tina looked at her hopefully and Lucy blushed.

'You're not. I—'

'Shame.' Tina pulled a face. 'In that case, I'll have a coffee.'

Lucy flicked on the kettle and stiffened as she heard the front door click. She reached for two mugs and met Tina's eyes.

'Did you have a good night?'

Lucy nodded. 'The best.'

But now it was over, and she couldn't even bear to think about it.

Sam wandered off to his bedroom to play with his toys and Tina moved closer, keeping her voice low.

'Michael and Nick will have Joel's blood if he hurts you.'

Lucy gave a soft smile. 'He hasn't hurt me.'

Joel Whittaker had never been anything but honest with her. If there was hurt to come—which there undoubtedly would be—then it wasn't his fault. She'd gone into last night with her eyes wide open.

Remembering the way he'd looked at her as they'd made love made her blush, and Tina sighed.

'It's so romantic. I just knew you were the one for Joel, right from the first moment.'

Lucy looked at her, startled. 'What do you mean?'

'Oh, come on, Lucy!' Tina's voice was soft. 'Since when did Joel go out of his way to be friends with a woman? The answer is never. But he did with you. He feels differently about you.'

Lucy swallowed. 'You're wrong.'

Tina frowned. 'He didn't say anything to you last night?'

'No.'

'What about this morning when you woke up?'

Lucy blushed. 'You woke us up.'

'Oh, no!' Tina pulled an apologetic face. 'And you haven't even had time to talk?'

Why was everyone so obsessed with talking? She couldn't see that there was anything to talk about.

Lucy put her coffee down and dredged up a smile. 'Look—can we just leave it? Joel hasn't led me on, Tina. I knew exactly what sort of man he was when I—when—'

'When you let him make love to you.' Tina nodded thoughtfully. 'Well, don't give up. If he hasn't said those three little words yet, I'm quite sure he will. I'm sorry I came back when I did.'

After they'd finished their coffee Tina left, leaving Lucy to play with Sam.

But she couldn't concentrate. All she could think about was Joel and the way he'd made her feel.

Even if she were to never see him again, she knew she could never regret what had happened between them.

How could she?

He'd aroused feelings in her that she hadn't known she was capable of feeling. To have gone through life never knowing what true love felt like would have been incredibly sad.

But she knew now.

She knew exactly what true love felt like.

It was what she felt for Joel.

The asthma clinic was busier than ever, and Lucy saw a steady stream of patients right through until lunchtime.

'I still can't believe this is asthma.' Mrs Lambert was back again, having had a bad attack the week before. 'It's just a chest infection.'

'Has Dr Richard given you antibiotics?'

'Two lots.' Mrs Lambert sniffed. 'The first lot didn't work. Useless.'

Lucy gave a sympathetic smile. 'And the second lot?'

'Well, I'm feeling a lot better, but he insisted that I take steroids as well and increase my puffer.' She looked appalled. 'What do you think?'

Touched that Mrs Lambert trusted her so much, Lucy sat down next to her and took her hand.

'The steroids are to settle the inflammation in your lungs,' she explained. 'It will help ease your breathing until the infection settles. Once your chest is better we need to look at you again and maybe decrease the amount you're taking your puffers. But for now, keep doing what Dr Richard suggested.'

'I tried to walk to the shops yesterday,' Mrs Lambert told her. 'I nearly breathed my last.'

'The cold air will irritate your lungs. If you need to go out, wear a scarf over your mouth, and when you're indoors keep the heating on so that you're not breathing in cold air.'

Mrs Lambert frowned. 'What? Even at night?'

Lucy smiled. 'Yes, at night. It doesn't have to be high, just enough to take the chill away from the air that you're breathing in.'

'I suppose you're going to tell me not to go out next!'

Lucy shook her head. 'I think while you have a chest infection and it's this cold you'd be better off indoors if you can, but generally it's good to exercise when you have asthma. Exercising regularly can actually help your asthma improve. Walking is great. So is swimming.'

'Swimming!' Mrs Lambert looked at her in horror and then started to laugh. 'Have you any idea what I look like in a swimming costume?'

Lucy laughed too and gave her an impulsive hug. 'I bet you look great, Annie.'

They talked some more, and once Lucy was satisfied that Annie understood why she needed to increase her puffers she walked with her back to the waiting room.

'Results for you, Lucy.' Ros waved a handful of forms and Lucy took them and wandered back to the treatment room, reading them carefully.

Halfway down the pile was Penny's chlamydia result, and she noticed that it was positive.

Bother.

Worried that Penny might have been exposed to other infections that she hadn't been able to screen for, Lucy made a mental note to have one more attempt at trying to persuade her to attend the sexual health clinic.

Knowing that she needed to discuss the case with Joel, she braced herself and tapped on his door.

She hadn't seen him since Tina had disturbed them, and she was trying not to feel disappointed that he hadn't tapped on her door. She'd known the score. There was no point in moping about it.

Hearing his voice, she lifted her chin and walked in, armed with Penny's results.

He looked up from his computer, his expression difficult to read. 'Good morning.'

'I—good morning—Penny tested positive for chlamydia,' she said quickly, and he nodded.

'All right. Well, when she calls in for the result, ask her to make an appointment to see me. I'll give her a gram of azithromicin.'

'Do we need to swab her again to check that the antibiotics have worked?'

Joel shook his head. 'Not unless she's still got symptoms. But of course we don't know what else the girl might have caught. When I see her I'll try and persuade her to go to the clinic.' He stared at her for a long moment and then he gave a hesitant smile. 'Lucy, we really need to talk. About us being friends—'

'It's what we both want, Joel, you know that,' she said quickly, backing towards the door and glancing at her watch. 'Sam's going to a friend's to play after school so I'm working late today. Give me a knock when you get home.'

With that she left the room, uncomfortably aware that there was a tension between them that hadn't been there before.

Friends.

Joel couldn't believe that Lucy still only wanted to be friends after what they'd shared.

Had their night together really meant so little to her?

He'd made love plenty of times before, but he'd never experienced anything like the intensity of feeling he'd shared with Lucy.

So what did that mean?

He still wasn't sure, but he knew that it had nothing to do with friendship.

Joel looked up in surprise as Nick stormed into the room without knocking.

'Now what?' He looked at his brother with a weary smile, guessing what was coming.

Nick planted his fists on the desk and glared at him menacingly. 'Tina said you spent the night with Lucy on Saturday.'

Joel was silent for a moment and when he finally spoke his voice was soft. 'That is none of your business.'

'So it's true.' Nick shook his head in disbelief, a look of contempt in his eyes. 'Dammit, Joel, we warned you! How could you, man? She's a child!'

'She is not a child.' Joel remembered the soft curves and her incredibly excited response to his love-making. 'Inexperienced, maybe. A child, most definitely not.'

'Well, I hope you're pleased with yourself.' Nick glared at him. 'What was she? Just one more notch on your bedpost? You make me sick!'

'Hold on a moment.' Joel shot to his feet in a lithe movement, his voice a low growl as he struggled with his temper. 'She was not a notch on my bedpost.'

Nick lifted an eyebrow. 'No? What was she, then?'

The two brothers glared at each other and Joel swore under his breath.

'I didn't do anything she didn't want—'

Nick made an impatient sound. 'But you made her want it, Joel! You can charm the birds from the trees. I can't believe you used Lucy like that.'

Joel gritted his teeth. 'I did not use her!'

'You're telling me you want a proper relationship with her?'

Joel stared at his brother and then sat back down in his chair with a thump, realising with startling clarity that that was exactly what he wanted.

'There's nothing I'd like more,' he said wearily, a wry smile touching his mouth as he registered the astonishment on his brother's face. 'Ironic, isn't it? I finally meet Miss Right and she doesn't want anything to do with me. Or, to be more precise, she just wants to be my *friend*.'

Nick was staring at him in stunned silence. 'After what

happened at the weekend, she just wants to be your *friend?* Are you serious?'

'Completely serious.' Joel ran a hand over his face and sighed. 'And I don't know how to handle it, Nick.'

The anger faded from his brother's face, to be replaced by a hint of amusement. 'Are you seriously telling me that you've finally fallen for someone?'

Joel gave him a resigned look. 'Go ahead. Laugh.'

Nick shook his head slowly. 'I'm not laughing, I'm delighted. You couldn't have picked a better person to fall in love with—'

'Hold it.' Joel lifted a hand and interrupted him. 'Aren't you forgetting something here? I might be in love with her, but she certainly isn't in love with me. She doesn't want any more than friendship.'

Nick looked at him doubtfully. 'Are you sure you've got that right?'

'It's been her most commonly used word since Saturday night,' Joel drawled softly, tapping his fingers on the desk and trying to conceal just how unsettled and frustrated he was by the situation.

Nick frowned. 'You told her that you love her but she said that she wasn't interested in being anything but your friend?'

There was a long silence and then Joel cleared his throat and shifted awkwardly. 'Well, I may not have actually *said* that I love her. At least, not in so many words, but—'

'OK, hold it right there!' Nick lifted a hand and stopped him in mid-flow. 'If you didn't actually tell her that you love her, how do you expect the girl to know?'

Joel rubbed a hand over his jaw. 'Well, I don't know. I suppose—'

'Joel!' Nick's tone was exasperated. 'It's just three little words. Are they really so hard to say?'

Joel looked at him. 'I don't know,' he said softly. 'I've never tried. And I don't see the point now. Lucy's made it clear that she just wants us to be friends.'

'How can you be so totally blind?' Nick looked at him incredulously. 'Lucy Bishop is the kindest, most unselfish person any of us have ever met and she knows that you've got a serious problem with commitment. If you haven't actually *told* her that you love her she's assuming that she doesn't mean anything to you, and she doesn't want to put pressure on you by confessing her own feelings.'

'But—'

'When have you ever been seriously involved with a woman before?'

'Well, never, but—'

'And does Lucy know that?'

Joel thought for a moment. 'Yes. We had a long conversation about love. I admitted that I didn't know what love was.'

Nick rolled his eyes. 'There we are, then.'

Joel frowned. 'But that was before we—'

'Before you made love to her,' Nick finished softly. 'But you still haven't ever said those words, have you? It's time to tell her how you feel about her, Joel.'

Joel's shoulders tensed. 'But what if she doesn't feel the same way? She was badly hurt by Tim. I don't think she's keen to get involved with another man.'

Nick sighed. 'Joel, take it from me. The girl is in love with you. She's crazy about you, but she seems to have accepted you the way you are and she's putting on a brave face.'

'But—'

'Listen—take some brotherly advice for once in your life, will you?' Nick took a deep breath and ran his hands through his hair. 'Think long and hard about whether you really want to lose Lucy, because that's what's going to happen if you don't act quickly. Is one night with a woman like her really enough? Or even a hundred nights? Think, Joel! Because if you don't drag her into your cave quickly, someone else is going to do it. And they're going to do it soon. That girl is special, Joel. Really special.'

'I know that—'

'So come to your senses and ask her to marry you,' Nick said, his expression bleak. 'Before it's too late.'

With that he turned on his heel, leaving Joel staring after him.

Was Nick right?

Did Lucy really love him?

And was he ready to make a proper commitment for the first time in his life?

He was still mulling over his feelings when the door crashed open again and Michael dashed into the room, his face strained.

'Get yourself up to the hospital. Sam's had a serious asthma attack.'

Lucy hovered, white-faced and anxious, as the A and E team worked on Sam.

Seeing him struggling with his breathing so badly had left her shaking with panic. But she knew that there was nothing she could do except wait and let the team do their job.

'His resps are 55, pulse 140,' the nurse announced, adjusting the oxygen mask on Sam's face as she spoke.

Lucy stepped forward, unable to stay in the background any longer, and the doctor glanced at her, his expression sympathetic.

'This must be very distressing for you, Mrs Bishop.

Why don't you wait in the relatives' room?' he suggested quietly, but she shook her head, appalled at the thought.

'I can't leave him.'

The doctor hesitated and then nodded. 'All right, but if you change your mind…' He turned his attention back to Sam.

'His peak flow is less than forty per cent of his best reading and he's exhausted. I want to give him IV aminophylline over twenty minutes and then we'll set up a maintenance drip.' He looked at Lucy. 'Is he taking oral theophyllines?'

She shook her head and he turned back to the nurse. 'So we'll start with the loading dose and give him IV hydrocortisone as well. Have you called paeds?'

The nurse nodded. 'They're on their way.'

Lucy was shaking so badly she felt sick.

She could see just how severe the attack was. What if he didn't survive?

She understood better than most that asthma could still be a life-threatening illness.

'Lucy?'

She turned at the sound of her name and sagged with relief when she saw Joel standing in the doorway. He was out of breath and the expression on his face told her that he knew what had happened.

Michael must have told him. Dear Michael, who'd been by her side in the surgery when she'd taken the call from the mother of the friend that Sam had been playing with.

'It's Sam,' she told him, choking on the words. 'He's—' She broke off as tears clogged her throat, and Joel swore softly and strode into the room, pulling her against him and giving her a hug.

But he released her almost immediately and strode to Sam's bedside, his blue eyes sharp.

'What's the situation here?'

'Hi, there, Joel.' The casualty officer gave him a brief smile and Joel's face cleared.

'Harry? God, I'm pleased it's you.' He ran a hand through his hair. 'What's happening?'

'Well, he's having a pretty severe attack.' Harry handed Joel the chart, obviously not wanting to say too much in front of Sam. 'I've just given a loading dose of amino-phylline IV and we're setting up a drip now.'

Joel looked up from the chart. 'What are his sats like?'

'All right, actually,' the nurse said, checking the monitor. 'Ninety-six per cent now.'

'He's responding to treatment,' Harry murmured. 'Keep up the high-flow oxygen—great.'

Two more doctors bustled into the room. Harry introduced them as the paediatricians and then discussed the case with them while Joel listened.

'Do we know what caused it?'

They all looked at Lucy and she shook her head. 'No. He was playing at a friend's house.'

She couldn't imagine what would have triggered such a severe attack.

They all worked together and finally they announced that he was well enough to be transferred to the ward.

Still desperately worried, Lucy caught Joel's arm. 'Will he be all right?' She bit her lip. 'I've lost track of what they've been saying.'

He slipped an arm around her shoulders and pulled her against him. 'He's stable now and he's improving all the time. They're going to measure his peak flow every fifteen minutes for the time being and measure his sats. They're trying to keep his oxygen saturation above ninety-two per cent, and so far it's fine.'

SARAH MORGAN 183

Lucy tried not to look at Sam's pale little face—or the oxygen mask—as they wheeled him to the paediatric ward.

As they settled Sam into a bed, she turned to look at Joel. 'Thank you for coming.'

He gave her an odd look. 'I came as soon as I heard. I'm sorry I wasn't with you from the beginning. It must have been a nightmare.'

She nodded her head and then moved forward to hold Sam's hand as they made him comfortable.

Joel crouched down in front of her and lowered his voice. 'You're as white as a sheet, Lucy. Why don't you go and get yourself a coffee and I'll stay with him?'

Lucy shook her head immediately. 'I can't leave him,' she said firmly, and he gave a sigh.

'In that case, let me bring a cup of coffee to you.'

Lucy looked at the nurse. 'Is coffee allowed on the ward?'

The nurse hesitated. 'Not generally, but you look as though you need one so I'll turn a blind eye.'

Over the course of the evening Sam continued to improve, and when the lights went out on the ward Lucy stroked his arm gently.

'What happened at your friend's house, darling? What games did you play?'

He mumbled something and she moved the oxygen mask slightly so that she could hear him.

'I said we didn't really play a game. I cuddled the dog a lot.'

Lucy gasped and she and Joel exchanged glances.

'A dog.' The nurse came up behind them and nodded. 'All right, now we know what the little chap has to avoid in the future.'

'None of his friends in London had a dog,' Lucy said. 'I didn't even know it was a problem.'

Joel gave her shoulder a reassuring squeeze. 'Don't blame yourself. You weren't to know that pet hair was a trigger for him. Children with asthma react to different things. But we probably need to keep an eye on it in the future.'

She looked at him, wondering if he realised that he'd just said 'we'.

Telling herself not to read anything into it, she settled herself down for a long night by Sam's bedside.

Sam was kept in hospital for two days, and by the time they finally discharged him, Lucy was exhausted.

Joel came to collect them both, tall and broad-shouldered as he strode onto the ward. He looked sexily dishevelled as if he hadn't slept much either, which he probably hadn't, she reflected. After all, he'd spent most of the time on the ward with her and Sam, only leaving to honour his commitments to the surgery.

'He's going to be fine,' she said wearily, tucking a strand of dark hair behind her ear. 'We've got an appointment to come back in a couple of weeks.'

Joel scooped Sam into his arms and carried him to the car while she followed close behind, clutching all his medication.

They drove back to the flat in silence and Lucy let herself in, suddenly terrified of being on her own with Sam.

What if he had another attack?

Lucy turned to Joel, suddenly hesitant. 'Are you in tonight? It doesn't matter if you're not,' she said quickly, 'it's just that—'

'I'm staying here tonight,' he said immediately, giving her a smile that indicated he was aware of her fears. 'But he's going to be OK, Lucy. You're not going to need me.'

Oh, she needed him! And not just because of Sam...

She settled Sam in bed, and once he was asleep she went to find Joel, who was cooking supper.

'I wanted to thank you,' she said softly, her eyes slightly shy as she watched him from the doorway. 'You said that you'd never been anyone's friend before, and I just wanted to say that for someone with no experience you've done a great job. I think you've been the best friend that anybody could ever have or want to have.'

He was suddenly very still and his expression was guarded.

'Right. I wanted to talk to you about that.'

'About being friends?' She looked at him guiltily. 'I've imposed, haven't I? Y-you don't want to be friends any more.'

Joel abandoned his cooking and walked towards her, his expression serious. 'No. I don't want to be friends, but you haven't imposed. Far from it.'

'Then why can't we be friends?'

'Because that isn't the way I feel about you.' He put two fingers under her chin and lifted it, his blue eyes searching. 'You once asked me if I'd ever been in love.'

She swallowed. 'And you said no.'

'That's right. I did say no.' He nodded slowly, his thumbs gently stroking the smooth skin of her cheeks. 'But now I want you to ask me that question again.'

She stared at him, suddenly unable to speak, and he gave a slight smile.

'Ask me, Lucy.'

'Have you ever been in love?' She stumbled over the words as she always did when she was embarrassed about something, and he tilted her face so that she had no alternative but to look at him.

'Yes, I have,' he said softly. 'I was afraid that if it ever came my way I wouldn't recognise it. But I did, Lucy. I did recognise it. It took me a while, but I got there in the end.'

Her lips were parted but her breathing was shallow. 'What are you saying?'

His eyes darkened. 'I'm saying three words that I've never said before,' he said slowly, bending his head and kissing her gently on the mouth. 'I'm saying that I love you. And I'm taking a chance here because I have no idea how you feel about me. You keep saying that you want us to be friends, but is that really what you want? People keep telling me that you love me too. Is it true, Lucy?'

She was silent for a long moment and then she nodded slowly, hope slowly building inside her. 'Of course I love you. I thought it was obvious.'

'Not to me.'

She smiled at him uncertainly. 'But I'm useless at hiding how I feel, and you've had so much experience with women.'

'But no experience at all with love,' he pointed out, a wry smile touching his firm mouth. 'Until now.'

He reached into his pocket and pulled out a small silver box which he handed to her.

'I'm probably not doing this properly, but I want you to marry me, Lucy. Quickly. Before we waste any more time.'

She stared at the box stupidly. 'You want to marry me?'

'Definitely.' His voice was husky and very male. 'That night we spent together—it's never been that way with anyone before. When we woke up in the morning there was so much I wanted to say to you but we didn't have a chance to talk and then you seemed determined that our relationship wouldn't change.'

She looked at him in wonder. 'I thought that the last thing you wanted was commitment.'

'So did I.' His voice was soft. 'But I was wrong. You told me that I'd shown you that there are plenty of things in life left to discover. I suddenly realised that I didn't want you discovering those things with anyone but me. That was when I realised that I loved you.'

'And what about Sam?'

Joel smiled and kissed her gently. 'I love Sam and I'll be the best daddy I can possibly be to him—if he'll have me. I suppose I ought to propose to him, too, as I'm marrying both of you.'

'I don't think there's any doubt he'll say yes,' Lucy said, and his eyes searched hers.

'And what about you, Lucy? You haven't answered me yet.' He touched her cheek. 'Are you saying yes?'

She stared down at the box in her hand and opened it cautiously, gasping when she saw the stunning diamond ring nestling in the centre.

'Oh, Joel. It's beautiful...'

'And so are you.' He took the ring out of the box and slipped it onto her finger. 'And I'm still waiting for an answer. Are you going to marry me?'

'I certainly am, Dr Whittaker.' She stood on tiptoe and kissed him gently, her eyes full of love. 'I certainly am.'

Modern Romance™
...seduction and
passion guaranteed

Tender Romance™
...love affairs that
last a lifetime

Sensual Romance™
...sassy, sexy and
seductive

Blaze Romance™
...the temperature's
rising

Medical Romance™
...medical drama on
the pulse

Historical Romance™
...rich, vivid and
passionate

27 new titles every month.

*With all kinds of Romance for
every kind of mood...*

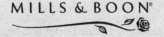

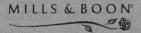

MILLS & BOON®

Medical Romance™

DEAR DOCTOR by Meredith Webber

Kirsten is engaged – sort of – to handsome rancher Grant. So what if playboy paediatrician Josh Phillips broke her heart? She's over it – and over him. Kirsten wants commitment, the one thing Josh can't give her. So why has her engagement done nothing at all for Kirsten's heart...and punched a hole in Josh's?

SURGEON ON CALL by Alison Roberts

Joe Petersen is a skilled surgeon – unfortunately, when it comes to being a dad he's a complete amateur! Joe's working with emergency consultant Fliss Munroe, and he wants her to be more than a colleague. What better way to get her interest than to recruit her to plan the best ever birthday party for a five-year-old girl!

THE DOCTOR'S ADOPTION WISH
by Gill Sanderson

When Nurse Jane Hall returns from California to help Dr Cal Mitchell take care of their orphaned niece, his life, his plans and his emotions are thrown into disarray. Jane might be a wanderer at heart, but Keldale is her home – and if Cal could only admit that he's fallen in love with her she just might stay for ever...

On sale 7th February 2003

Available at most branches of WH Smith, Tesco, Martins, Borders, Eason, Sainsbury's and all good paperback bookshops.

0103/03a

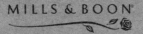

MILLS & BOON

Medical Romance™

DR MICHAELIS'S SECRET *by Margaret Barker*

An emergency rescue on Ceres Island has recent
arrival Staff Nurse Sara Metcalfe working with local
doctor Michaelis Stangos – and from the moment she
sees him diving into the waves she's hooked. But
Sarah senses he's hiding a painful secret. A secret
that's holding him back from what could be a perfect
relationship...

THE FAMILY PRACTITIONER *by Leah Martyn*

Life is pretty uneventful for Joanne, working at the
local clinic – until her teenage son Jason comes home
with an outrageous request that sends Joanna
marching off to see just what Dr Matthew McKellar is
up to! Suddenly her life is in chaos. She's got a
new job, with Matt as her new boss – and as her
new lover...

HER CONSULTANT BOSS *by Joanna Neil*

Dr Megan Llewellyn couldn't work out what she felt
most for her boss, consultant Sam Benedict –
exasperation or desire! Was he hiding an attraction
to her that was as intense as hers for him? When a
fire destroyed her home and Megan found herself
living with Sam she quickly found her answer!

On sale 7th February 2003

*Available at most branches of WH Smith,
Tesco, Martins, Borders, Eason, Sainsbury's
and all good paperback bookshops.*

0103/03b

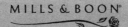

2 FREE

books and a surprise gift!

We would like to take this opportunity to thank you for reading this Mills & Boon® book by offering you the chance to take TWO more specially selected titles from the Medical Romance™ series absolutely FREE! We're also making this offer to introduce you to the benefits of the Reader Service™—

- ★ FREE home delivery
- ★ FREE gifts and competitions
- ★ FREE monthly Newsletter
- ★ Exclusive Reader Service discount
- ★ Books available before they're in the shops

Accepting these FREE books and gift places you under no obligation to buy, you may cancel at any time, even after receiving your free shipment. Simply complete your details below and return the entire page to the address below. *You don't even need a stamp!*

YES! Please send me 2 free Medical Romance books and a surprise gift. I understand that unless you hear from me, I will receive 4 superb new titles every month for just £2.55 each, postage and packing free. I am under no obligation to purchase any books and may cancel my subscription at any time. The free books and gift will be mine to keep in any case.

M3ZEA

Ms/Mrs/Miss/Mr ....Initials...............................
BLOCK CAPITALS PLEASE

Surname ....

Address ....

....

....Postcode...............................

Send this whole page to:
UK: FREEPOST CN81, Croydon, CR9 3WZ
EIRE: PO Box 4546, Kilcock, County Kildare (stamp required)

Offer valid in UK and Eire only and not available to current Reader Service subscribers to this series. We reserve the right to refuse an application and applicants must be aged 18 years or over. Only one application per household. Terms and prices subject to change without notice. Offer expires 30th April 2003. As a result of this application, you may receive offers from Harlequin Mills & Boon and other carefully selected companies. If you would prefer not to share in this opportunity please write to The Data Manager at the address above.

Mills & Boon® is a registered trademark owned by Harlequin Mills & Boon Limited.
Medical Romance™ is being used as a trademark.